GOOD HEART

GOOD HEART

BY
DEREK A. KAMAL

ARTWORK BY
JACOB HUNT

SHORELESS SKIES

For the girls

1. CIDER

When a man decides to face the desert, to challenge that wretched span of God's handiwork, he puts something on the line. It's neither neither just nor always his skin. Ways have been found around that. Clothes for the skin, hats for the shade, good supply of water and beasts to carry it all. Even beasts at home in the sand and the heat. Like as not it won't be man's skin doesn't make it out of the desert. It's something else. And sometimes a man makes it out whole, but carries something back. Something meant for elsewhere.

Right now, he's thinking only of his skin. Shuffling down the miles of sand and dirt and heat on his own two feet, sure he'd make it but equally sure he'd be just as happy somewhere shady. Sits under a rock for a few minutes, takes his last few swigs of water and wipes the sweat away. Rocks are a good sign. On the way in, he'd left rocks about a day away and all turned to golden orange sand before he'd started the return trip. Rocks are everywhere now, standing their long defeat against the desert. He's close. So close that after another hour of walking he sees it. The town's just a square, walled off against intruders, but to him it's like a beautiful woman holding her arms wide.

Last few miles are a beast. Thirst sets in, fatigue, worry. Sold the deception too hard, perhaps. A needless trip to the desert. Can't quite recall if he'd done the right thing or if he should have just done what was asked of him. No tricks for once in his life, just follow orders. Hell, he was never very good at following orders direct and as the town becomes real, as he can almost touch those dun-gray walls, something strikes his mind. Can't say what it is; epiphany, dehydration, the good Lord trying to peck him on the shoulder. But it's there. A curious feeling of realization without anything to realize; the moment you're sure you had a profound dream in your sleep but you just can't remember what it was. Best to leave that one alone, trust it just might come back if it's supposed to.

He grips the thing, the pendant resting against his chest, round his neck, and moves on, wondering if he ought've done what Jack had paid him to. Smirks at that, the bizarre man called Jack; nobody round here named Jack, but he'd not asked into it.

Walks slowly through the crowded streets somewhere on the eaves of the Sahara, receives countless odd looks for his lumbering gait and the blade on his hip. They clear a path for him, but it's not always wide enough. Summer sun beats down upon his head. Rest are cloaked or wearing soft hoods or even turbans; his is bare, save for that short, straight hair.

Hair like that make a woman swoon, he'd heard once. Lawrence'd told him that. What a man that Lawrence was. Also had told him brown skin was a grand thing, maybe even better than white skin. Asked him what he thought about skin.

'Who's got the time to care about skin?' he'd asked.

'Just about everyone I ever met,' said Lawrence.

Now, however, he'd shave all that hair off and trade in his white skin for something to cover his dome. Jack had hats. Jack's probably the wealthiest man he ever met, no doubt wealthier than anyone else in this town.

Ω

A few days in the desert, even well-provisioned, takes it out of a man. He's looking for shade and something cool to put down his throat, but all he's finding is more shoulders to knock into, more old donkey dung to evade, more market stalls selling things he's got no interest in. He flicks at his beard and winces; finger grazed a patch of sunburn on his cheek. Soon he'd be as brown as all these folks that stare him down, going on about their day selling chickens or roots or cider. Cider!

The sight of it makes his heart pound a bit harder. Not the best choice for the thirstful, but sweet and boozy.

He paws his way between some ladies who don't move and who stare at his blade, turns round a pottery stall, and bellies up to another. This one's got liquid gold on the shelves. Doesn't bother with words, just holds up two fingers, checks out the birds overhead. Gulls, maybe. He was close to the Sea, after all. The cider-man with the thick moustache puts half-full glasses on the bar of the stall that's made to look like a bar. He sips and sighs and notes that he's the only one there. Maybe these people don't drink. He hadn't taken time to check in on the local culture or poke a head into their churches when the caller called. Looks up at the sky again. Maybe they don't drink before noon. Maybe here's a foolhardy businessman peddling booze in a land that can't buy it.

It's not real cold, and not as good as wine, but cool enough and sweet enough to satisfy. The little brown cider-man smiles and nods and says something he can't understand, pointing to the one empty glass. He flashes a thumbs-up. It's good and the thumb says so anywhere in the world. Finds himself wondering where these apples even came from. Across the Sea, no doubt.

Wasn't too long ago he was across that Sea, roping horses. The work was good, the sun hot, the food tasty. The wine was best; they chilled it there across the Sea, put fruit in it. Perfect thing after a hot day out ranging and moving horses from here to there. That struck him as real funny, how a man could make a living by moving horses or cattle from one place to another. Things're always moving, why not capitalize on it? Just like a man. Horses were beautiful there, though, 'cross the Sea. Not as beautiful as back home, but the country was lovely and the horses matched.

It was after a long move over low mountains, low when one thinks of the Rockies, to a ranch on the far east side that one of his companions made the suggestion.

Ω

They were tired, but the rancher fed them well and after his third glass he went from tired to drowsy. The space was nice, clean. He half-wished he could scoop up the little house and dump it back home, but it would stand out too much. A simple log house would have suited him right as can be.

'Where you going after this?' his fellow cowboy had said.

'Can't rightly say, Abel.' He'd been thrilled to hear he spoke English, even if it was rough. No more rough than any other language I'd ever spoke, he thought.

'Go south, by the Sea. I believe you like it there!'

He remembered his friend's small, black eyes, how he seemed to sweat constantly. No doubting why; it was hot as hell there, but no hotter than it is here.

Ω

Nice and shady and restful at the cider-stall, though, and he thinks he ought to sit there for at least an hour, gather his wits and rest his dogs, but there's work afoot. Best get it done, or else a trip through the desert was for nothing. Nothing except a sunburn, a dead mule, and a lost hat. Should've listened and kept a turban, he thinks. Turban can't keep out what plagues a mind alone for miles without a thing but sand to comfort him. Shudders at that, the memory of darkness among unending dunes; dark as any place he's ever known, as any place the sun ever shone upon.

Nights were the worst. Then the darkness was made real and even the stars, bright as man can see, only float to contrast the cold and night-shadows and blink with the nightly noises. Remembers hearing something some time about the devil coming from the desert and the touch of those evenings gave him a half-belief. Nothing for it but to finish what's already done.

So he stands up, notes that he's about a head taller than the cider-man and downs his beverage. He's not a tall man by any means, just taller than these folks somehow. Makes to tip his hat but finds it's still missing, so he waves instead. Cider-man waves back. Good, he thinks, a new friend.

The little town's just that, a little town. Mud-brick walls hold mud-brick houses, turrets along those walls just might keep out invaders or crazed barbarians, but who would want to invade a little dump like this? So, with an easy way out of the dangers of the world, these folks go about their days, raising camels and selling cider. The little domed houses in the little town make him a little nostalgic, like a little town was all a man needed. Set up shop outside a little town and the little world would fall right into place. Or buy a little ranch. This is what goes through his head as he stomps his soft old boots along, wondering if he listens just right he can hear the sea.

The Sea! The Sea!

He's chuckling to himself now, thinking he's far from home and buzzing from cider and worn out from the burning sun that won't back down. Now's the time to find Jack, he thinks. Talk to Jack and then get gone, get to where the sun ain't so bright and a man can have a rest without snorting dust up his nostrils. Where that is he's not quite sure, but it's likely across the Sea.

2. JACK

Jack. Jack's a liar, but he's no sneak. Can't trust a man named Jack from this part of the world because there are no Jacks from this part of the world. Jack's fine out west, beyond the ocean a world away, but here? Jack's a foreign name. So when a man who looks like a local, talks like a local, and eats like a local calls himself Jack you can know that man's got a thing or two for hiding. Figured his right name would be too much of a mouthful for a non-native to handle.

He likes that, in his way. Makes him feel like he's got a friend besides cider-man back yonder. Makes it feel a little like home; just a little, mind, but a little can go a long way out here in the desert. If he stops to think, however, he knows Jack's no friend. So he's stepping now, hoping Jack's got a big glass of water sitting on his nice table for him. Cider's taking effect, but it's not strong stuff. Just enough to remind him that it's cider he's been drinking. That loose feeling makes the walk across town pleasant enough. These aren't city streets, so all the pleasantry as can be extended he'll take. This town's all mud-brick, all brown except for the fine blue scarves and veils, red robes and shirts the people wear. Even a little green and purple mixed in. They're all going somewhere but that somewhere's not too far away. Town can't be more than a mile across, if that.

Sometimes he thinks the town smells like fear, like something bad's on its way, or the people think that something bad is riding them down. Smelled like that in the desert. Can't put his finger on it. Still, he thinks, better here than out there.

Town's got little to set one street apart from the next. It's a town full of twins and cousins. Might be a barrel on one street, some clothes hanging to dry the next, but in the end it's all short, mud-brick huts and in a small town full of one room, mud-brick huts, Jack's house is a mansion. Three rooms, high ceilings, strong enough for a patio on the roof. Patio's even got a hookah.

Ω

Jack's a tough character. Not much known about him, save that he made his fortune away in foreign parts and runs this little town now as part of a quiet, tidy retirement. No telling if he was raised here, liked it here, or just threw a dart on a map and found this little town to hide from the world. Things as they are, Jack's the only game in town for a rugged white wanderer to make a bit of coin.

They'd met happenstance when he made up his mind to have his little adventure in the desert. Were as if Jack'd been waiting on him, expecting him, knowing some Westerner would be walking off the dock on a Sunday's afternoon (if that's what day it was). And he'd taken Jack's hand in his as if he knew what it meant, that it was meant to be. After some smooth words and a hill of courtesy, he was at Jack's place enjoying the cool, wondering if he should have brought his sixgun across the sea. The water was good, smelled clean, the English was better; frustration of pantomiming every little thing'd left him worn down.

'Why have you come so far to our little town here?'

Jack liked to be direct, though he surely didn't care much about whatever answer was about to come.

'Work,' he said.

Jack laughed at that. 'Work! Of course! It is what all teeny little desert villages are for!'

'Just heard there was big things across the Sea.' Wasn't totally true, but true enough for Jack.

Jack liked that more, nodded slow and thoughtful. 'That is true. The desert is all of wonder and legends. That is wise of you. But I cannot say I trust a strange vagabond.'

Vagabond was a big word for someone who didn't grow up speaking English. 'Can't say I trust a little brown man from the desert named Jack.'

Jack laughed again. 'Very good! Well, since we are not trusting each other, I will give you my business.'

And so it went for a few days, constant errantry for Jack. Money wasn't bad and it got better when Jack tossed a small cloth, heavy with some item, over the table.

'What's this?'

'A burden,' Jack said.

Pregnant silence, as they say. 'That's it?'

'Through the desert, up the coast and such. Away. Then you throw it into the Sea. It will be happy there.'

He smirked then, wondering what would be happy in the Sea, wondered how literal old Jack here was being and how tricky he was, or if his English just made him sound trickier than the real man. No, Jack was tricky. He flopped the cloth open, saw the thing and wondered some more.

'What is it?'

Jack only shook his head and a strong-looking fellow escorted him out.

That was four days ago. He knocks, just twice, just enough to get the door open. The same tall, strong-looking fellow opens the door. He's wearing a long black robe, short bushy beard, and a frown. Got a sword on his hip and a rifle slung over his shoulder; even the gunstrap's black. He goes to step in but the strong man steps in front of him.

'Remember me?' he says. The strong man's like a statue, staring at him, sizing him up. Soon as he starts thinking trouble, Jack's voice yells something in the local tongue and the strong man stands down. Good thing, too. Strong man looks strong...and dangerous. And just like that, Jack is yelling for him, telling him to sit down and 'how the hell are ya?'. There is water.

'Must say, you gave me some kind of scare,' says Jack. His accent makes his talk all the more hilarious. Jack was not named Jack by his mother. Never even been to places where men were named Jack, but a man's got to be called something.

'Gave myself a scare, must say.'

'Well I sometimes think you are not caring about yourself as much as I am. I think you toss yourself into the wind like a handful of leaves,' says Jack.

'You have leaves here?'

'Of course we do, smart fellow! More across the sea, certainly, but we have our trees here. It is not all just sand and rock, come come! You speak without thinking.'

'Anyways.'

'Anyways. It is done, then? No trouble?'

'Not too much trouble.' He leans back, stretches those long legs out and thankfully gulps some water.

'Come, come! Surely there is more to the telling than just that.'

'Just lost myself a mule is all.'

'Mules are replaced easily. My little trinket, not so much.'

'Anyone wants that replaced'll be looking a long time.'

'Long time. Do we any of us have long time? No. But maybe longer for me now.' Jack gets a look in his eyes, the kind another man doesn't want to see. 'Okay. Your pay is due then.'

'Second half of it anyway.' He sits up a little straighter, reminds himself where he keeps his blade, wishes he had a gun. But no, Jack wasn't a sneak like that, just a liar. Of course his 'little trinket' was much more than that; no man pays a stranger, a foreigner, good money to dump something in the Sea for no good reason. That's what hit him after a few days in the desert; why lose this thing forever in the Sea when one can lose it among a trusted associate? Then that associate can sell it for another payday.

Jack stands up and straightens his v-neck tunic. It's brown. A brown shirt for a brown man in a brown town. There are pictures on the wall, pictures of the land, the sea, little people he doesn't know. If Jack can move a little quicker I can buy all the pictures I want, he thinks. Finally Jack makes good. He wipes a little sweat from his bald head and there's a sack on the table now, full of things that clink.

He looks inside, picks one up and gives it a good bite. Gold alright. Jack is no sneak.

'Where will you go now? For go you must,' says Jack.

'Can't say,' he replies. Jack's accent makes it hard not to laugh. Sounds more like a character from funny books than a big, rich, powerful man. Guess it don't take too much to be big and rich and powerful in a small town in the desert.

'Go,' says Jack again, nodding to the wide world beyond

his mud-brick house. It is strangely cool in here. 'Go and make a life. You have money now, enough to last you some time. Go find a woman, farm the land or something.'

'Why young Jack, I'd think you were trying to get rid of me. Am I of no more use to you?'

Jack's got that look back in his eyes, like he's fighting a voice in his head whispering murder. 'You are not of more use to me. So, where will you go?'

'Don't think I'll be telling you that, Jack, even if I knew.'

'Good!'

He stands up slowly, not taking either eye off of Jack. Jack's no sneak, but all the same...can't be too careful. Dying alone in the desert far from home is no man's idea of a proper passing. Time to take the money and be on his way; rest and get back to find what was lost.

'Good day to you, Jack. I do hope we meet again.'

'Insha'Allah,' says Jack.

He goes to tip his hat again, catches himself and scratches his bare head instead. Smooth move, quick thinking. How I got to be so rich, he muses. Wants to blush but doesn't. Instead he turns and moves with purpose, his soft boots flapping against the dirt floor. Strong man gives him a dirty look, but strong man don't know how quick he could die.

3. Orphans

Back outside now. Things are winding down with the sun. He's looking round for a place to stay; been years since he was in such a town at night alone. Previous nights he'd camped at Jack's. Can't remember if they have inns or hotels or hostels or the like, but he hopes they do. He's got an ache in his back and one in each foot; thought, maybe, he'd dodge some saddle sores, the one good thing about his mule dying, but instead he's got sore feet, too. The mud-brick houses are coming alive now. Families sitting down for dinner, he thinks and gets a little forlorn, a little nostalgic like. Lights are on in there, dim but visible. Little candles probably. No fireplaces here, just little ovens like warm hearts pumping blood through homes.

Didn't have such a warm heart pumping back in his home, no real home at all. Hence his forlorn goings.

He hears someone yelling in the local tongue and comes to. It's Cider-man, still there behind his cart at the edge of the market square, still smiling like a fool. Takes a smile to make money, he thinks, and waves back. Cider-man keeps on waving him down, using his hat like a banner, like he doesn't know he's been seen.

I'm gonna need that hat if I'm gonna survive in this place long, he thinks. Hot even with the sun setting.

Before he can mosey over and waste his newfound wealth on cider, he notices something. Folks are moving about quickly now, heads down, eyes on their feet. Gotta be a ghost came through or the like. More than one merchant, who'd been hawking his wares like a crier, is now scurrying off home. Evening prayer, he thinks, but hears no call.

So he moves across the town, dirt and sand sliding under his feet. He's been Cider-man's only customer today; times are hard and people in these parts put alcohol last on their lists, if they put it on there at all. No, he thinks, I won't be finding any bar in this town, not even a hotel bar. Cider's as good as anything. So he bellies up again, dirty buttons brushing up against the cart. Cider-man's brushing his moustache out, wiping his hands on his vest. He don't really look like a local. His hat tells the tale; he's a trader, maybe, come from over the Sea. Maybe a local man, caught a glimpse of life outside dirt huts and wanted a piece. Doesn't matter. Cider-man's holding up two fingers quizzically, like a child who learned a new trick. He shakes head, wraps his hand around Cider-man's until just one of his fingers are sticking up. Cider-man chuckles, looks uncomfortable, and pours.

'I need a hat,' he says between sips. He taps his head to emphasize the point. Cider-man nods, narrows those big brown eyes like he's pondering a question beyond his station, says something unintelligible, tries again: 'Hair…off?'

'No…no, I don't need no haircut,' he says, amused and annoyed. 'Hat!' Now he's pointing at Cider-man's bowler cap. Yep, gotta be a merchant.

'Oh!' Cider-man's mumbling again in the local tongue, or some other language. 'No, my.'

'Where can I buy a hat, then?' He points to the cap, then looks around the town in the fading light of dusk, pantomiming his search.

'No here,' says Cider-man.

He pulls his payday out of his pocket, smirking like a jackal. Starts laying coins on the table. Cider-man's smiling himself now, though he looks more a dog than a jackal. Once the fifth coin hits the table the hat hits his head and Cider-man's snatched up his payday.

More'n he's seen in a long time and more than I'd ever pay for a hat, he thinks.

His mind's changing, he can feel it, so he downs the cider before he demands a refund from Cider-man.

Quickly, he asks his new best friend, 'Where can I sleep?' He folds his hands together and lays his head on them like a cheap pillow. Cider-man thinks and points away to his right, beyond some more mud-brick houses towards the far wall of town. He tips his new cap, gladly, though it don't feel right on the short brim.

Bet I look an ass, he thinks. But who's here to care?

The hostel, for it was no proper inn, was just a long house, like the rest of town but longer. Longer for more beds. He shoves the blanket covering the door aside, walks in and finds it empty. The odd feeling from before follows him inside like a shadow; no shadows after dusk, though. He narrows his eyes, has a look round. Gotta make sure the dim light isn't playing with him. No, there's nothing here but a big empty. It's late, about the time an inn would fill up in decent places, but this isn't really decent places. The hostel looks like it's seen a stampede or two of horses or cows or bigger beasts. Town outside was so quiet and calm he never thought to see something like it in these parts, but there it is; owner's lying dead, draped over a table like a big, wet blanket. He adjusts his new hat, gives it a little tip, and walks on quiet like, bare fingers grazing over dusty tables, leaving streaks. He'd hung up his spurs when his mule died and good thing, too; any noise would've been like a marching band in the cold, dull quiet. Best not disturb the dead.

Still silent, save for the creaking of the dusty lamp above him, swaying drunk. Still silent save for that scuffle he just heard. Behind him. He spins, goes for his blade but there's nothing there. Nothing but a table turned over where the others were upright.

'Come on out,' he says. Nothing comes out.

Damn fool, he says to himself. But then he hears it again, steps over quickly and quietly, swears he's gonna kill that rat for scaring him, then swears the same upon the creaky floorboards that mean to give him away. He stands before the overturned table. It's round, probably used for poker if they play poker in this part of the world. Draws his blade, puts his foot on the round piece of wood, four foot across, kicks it over.

There's no rat, just a girl. She's cowering, crying, got her hands up over her head but he can still see the trail her tears carved through the dirt on her face. He swears again, this time at nobody, and makes his blade go away, sits on the floor in front of her. Best calm down before addressing her, so he runs a hand through his beard and breaths deep, wincing again when his finger grazes the sunburn on his cheek.

'Alright, kid?' It's a stupid question but nothing else springs to mind. She's mumbling, sputtering something in the local tongue. He shakes his head, can't understand. The girl calms visibly. Her hands are down now and she takes a long, hard look at this new stranger. Sees she's dainty, brown with piercing eyes, a lady-to-be, or would be if she hadn't just found hell come knocking at her door. She points and tries again, points at the dead bartender. 'Father,' she says. 'Father!' and starts crying anew.

He bows his head, feels his heart flutter, feels the pain well up behind his eyes, and then makes it go away. He nods quick, two bouncing nods, then looks at the poor girl again. 'Come on, kid,' he says. 'I'll look after you tonight.'

She looks scared still, real scared, but something clicks in her head. Something like trust. Not knowing why, she takes his hand.

They're cozied up now, each sitting on a bed in the dark corner. They don't dare to put on any lights. Took him the better part of an hour to calm her down; she wants no part in this place, no part. Wants to be outside, away from her dead father and her smashed up home.

He'd at least put her father's body in the adjoined room, covered him up. They'd find a preacher, or whoever, tomorrow to see to his remains, but for tonight there was nothing doing but a good sleep. This girl wasn't about to sleep though.

'No! No! No!' she'd protested, and cursed him a thousand times in her own language. It didn't stop, even when he'd brought her a bucket of water and a rag to clean up. She'd sputter and curse at him between wipes or during.

'We got to stay here!' he'd said, wiping himself clean too. 'No good out in the dark, not with a little girl on my side. Can't find nobody like that out there. So we're sitting down and having a sleep!'

She wouldn't stop her shouting, bouncing back and forth between screaming and sobbing, until he feared somebody'd come looking. So he started shouting himself. It shut her up and now she's huddled on one of the little hostel beds, holding her knees and rocking, singing some sad song he doesn't understand. He loves her. Can't understand it, but he does.

'Orphans got to stick together,' he says, knowing she would not understand him. But she does somehow. She looks at him, big green eyes through ragged black hair. Understanding was there. She sings some more, and when she cries and can't sing any more he sings. He sings Old Susana, Camptown Races, Amazing Grace. Sings in a low, quiet voice. He even risks stroking her hair. She shivers, but does not protest. He stops anyway.

Orphan, he thinks, she's probably got a mom or some-such relation here. We'll sort it out in the morning.

Morning couldn't come quick enough. Whoever did this was out there. No doubt they'd be back, if they've any inkling their victim's daughter saw something. By God, he wants a gun.

4. EMMA

'Sean.' He's holding his hand to his chest like a salute. 'Sean.' He says it again and then gestures at the girl. She shakes her head.

'My name is Sean. What's your name? What do I call you, girl?'

She shakes her head again, eyes weighed down with great purple sacks. Didn't sleep a wink while he'd dozed all night. Couldn't fight it, not after a long trek and his heart nearly bursting out of his chest the day before. She's got no name, or she's got one she wants to forget.

Or she just don't understand you, he thinks.

'Emma,' Sean says. 'Had a sister called Emma once, not too long ago. Heard she's in Bixby last time I bothered to ask. You don't know what Bixby is. You don't know what Emma is either, do you?'

She nods. 'Emma.'

He smiles. 'Okay then. You be Emma, I'll be Sean.' There's a silence now, but not the kind of silence folks hate; just silence. Two humans looking at each other, seeing what's there, wondering if there's a right call to make, wondering at faces. And like that, it's broken.

'Got things you want to take? We're gone in five minutes.' No time to tease out the mystery of this little girl. How old was she? Twelve? Thirteen? Sean'd never been good with numbers like that. She seems calm, even too calm for a kid who's just seen her father shot down. He's wondering at that, how a man could be shot down in this sandcastle of a town and the gunshots not be heard from here to the Sea.

Sean'd found a burlap sack night before, same kind of sack he's carrying, and hands it to her now, gesturing around the room. She understands him just fine. Picks up a few things, wanders off to a chest stowed away in the corner and loads a few more into the bag. Nice place to keep things safe in a hostel, otherwise the guests might get to taking.

Ω

Emma's not scared of people. Life in a little house where others come to sleep in a little town had shown her a lot in her scant years, one of them being that people are just people. Even murderers. Here, people stayed as guests in the homes of others, so only those without places to stay came to this place. The foreigners and the strangers. Ones who could teach her bits and pieces of language until it was all one ugly tapestry without meaning or context.

There'd been the odd fight over the years, little scuffles by little people, until that one day of days when she was a little girl and some damn fool'd brought a gun to a knife fight. Emma could remember shouting, her father trying to bring the tone down without success. She could remember the stink of the men, sweaty with toil and fear; their robes would have told the tale but they were black. Just right for hiding sweat stains. She could remember the dim light coming through the windows and how she wished she could fly out of one of them and go somewhere else, somewhere where her father was big and strong and could have squashed these men like bugs.

A gunshot had pulled her back and one of the men was lying on the ground, moaning, clutching his belly. She hated it and wished again, prayed that God would take her away or just make her strong. But God took his own sweet time and her strength was years in coming. So she watched the man bleed and die, just like the others did. Just like her father would. Then they'd taken him away, the killer, and the village leader had chopped his head off. Then Emma got strong.

But all the strength of the desert wasn't enough to save her from what had happened the day before. She's got a brave face on, a nice mask to show this stranger how strong she is, but she's still spooked. If Sean knew what she knew he'd be spooked too.

Ω

They're moving now, said goodbye to her poor dad and now they're on the way across town. Dad'll be buried soon, so a hasty goodbye's alright for the time being. He wants to see Jack. Jack's got connections, knows people, knows English. He's got to know an undertaker as well as someone to take in this little girl. Sean's got a new life to start, much as he cares for the little orphan he can't have her slowing him down, not when there's wine and horses across the Sea and beyond and a fortune around his neck. It's early yet, sun's just barely peeping out, town smells like bread and smoke. He wonders if there's a baker open because he's starving. No food in the hostel, just bad dreams.

She's looking here and there, eyes darting around like a rabbit who's caught a whiff of fox. She's not so scared now, wary and cautious morelike. She's looking strong, like she's made a vow, like what happened yesterday was the devil and she cut the deal. Town's still asleep, mostly, but she's not buying it. Not buying the quiet that whispers words like 'safety' and 'rest'.

Sean stops and rubs his forehead, adjusts the new hat that just doesn't fit right. She shoots him an annoyed glance, like a bullet through the eye, but he's tapping his mouth now. 'Gotta eat', he says. Emma looks like she wants to slap him, would if her hands didn't shake so. She motions for him to wait but he acts like he doesn't get it. No way's he going to let her alone, so he follows her, up the street and around. Air's starting to make him think he's stuck in some oven somewhere, a wonderful place that's made of bread and grandma's cooking. And like that, a loaf of flat bread is warming his hand. Emma's ripped a bit off, muttering something in her language and gesturing that it's time to go. Sean sees the window sill, the basket, and wonders who in their right mind leaves bread to cool on the sill like a pie. Foreign ways, tasty bread.

They're moving again and so's the town, but none seem to be the wiser, no one showing a sign that murder's been done in their quiet little home. Do they not know or not care? Her head's down. Of the few treading here and there not a soul says a word, but they're looking. No, they're staring. Who's this white man with this little brown girl? The stares are like blows. They feel naked, exposed. Moving faster, faster, if only they could make it to Jack's there would be safety. When the stares start stinging they're there, banging on the door. Nothing. He bangs again. Nothing but an echo. No strong man, no Jack. He opens the door.

They're inside now. The mud-brick wall keeps out the stares. Just as cool and quiet as it had been the day before, only no one's home. Maybe Jack's fled and strong man's off the clock. They're looking now, hunting, going through this room then that one. It's big but small; no way Jack can't hear them so he's not here. But he's there, in the bedroom. Sean thanks God that Emma didn't find him first because it's grim. Jack's laying in bed, sound asleep but asleep forever. Throat's cut, blood's like another blanket on the small straw bed. His eyes are open.

'Stay away!' he calls, but she's coming anyway so he bars the door.

She's cursing again, out loud, in her language. Only word he can make out is 'Allah.' God. Was she cursing God? Swearing by Him? Did it matter? No. What matters is that people are dying and he doesn't want to be next, doesn't want this little girl to die by the sword or the gun or the knife or whatever these bastards are carrying.

Fear tries to sink in, grief too, but he shoves it away as best he can, lets them play out in his body but not his mind. Heart can beat a storm, hands can shake, mind's got to be clear.

Door's shut now. He doesn't remember doing it. They sit in the cool and the quiet, soak it in a little bit, hoping they can store it for later because the sun's up, the heat's waiting for them, and they know they're going to have to go and face it.

Ω

Still quiet. He's hoping an angel comes or something. She's got revenge on her mind, daggers in her eyes. If communication were a non-issue they'd be arguing; he for flight, she for the fight. But the words are hard and heavy, bricks they pass back and forth, and they're tired of the load so it's quiet. He's found the water and sucks it down greedily while she sips. They're looking for answers in the dirt floor, but he's getting more questions. Questions like, 'Why did a rich man like Jack not get proper floors put in?' Jack had been rich. Surely he'd kept some money round here somewhere. This doesn't look like a murder-and-steal job, just a plain old murder for reasons that were beyond Sean and his ken. He thanks God for that and starts looking and, quicker than he'd imagined, he starts finding.

All a new life takes is one big satchel of gold and he's found three, back in Jack's room under the bed. Poor, clever Jack. He had put in floorboards, but floorboards under the dirt under the bed. And under the floorboards hid lots and lots of money. It was easy to find and the ease confirmed his suspicions; the murderers weren't after his money. Doesn't make him feel any better. Who would kill him if not for his money? Who would Jack cross? Always played things close to the vest. Once again it was out of his reckoning. Had there been so much as a feeling of doubt linking this to his dubious job in the desert he ignored it.

Emma peers through the door, thinking she might cover her eyes rather than see the dead man but she just keeps her focus on Sean. And the gold. 'Get!' she calls. 'Get!'

'That's right, I get.' Got as much gold as he can carry loaded up.

'No!' she says. 'No! No!' She's stammering, falling in and out of her language, looking for the right word. 'Seal!' Not quite the right word, but it's more than Sean can say in the local tongue.

'Seal...steal? No, I don't steal.'

'Steal!'

'Jack was a friend of mine, you see. It's okay. I'm not taking all neither. Plenty here left for...whoever.'

Emma grumbles and paces, hands in her hair like she's going mad. 'Mal,' she says. 'Bad. Bad.'

'Well, little girl, this is our ticket to gone. I don't know if you've reckoned this, but whoever did your dad and Jack got to be looking for one or both of us. I got no gun and no wish to kill nobody, so I'm taking you away. Lest you got a mom somewhere in these parts. Mother?'

Emma shakes her head. That says enough. Nobody. He's got to press it, though, make sure. 'No family? No mother? No brother? No uncle, aunt, grandma?'

Shakes her again, whether or not she understood. Sean's starting to think she's got more English than she lets on, or she's a convincing liar. In the end, it's no matter. They're two sticks in the wind now, and Sean's at least got some notion of where things are blowing.

5. Strangers

'If we're going to make it to the coast we need some kind of animal to ride.'

They're outside now with no place to go. They're back outside with the stares and the trouble and the threat of murder lurking around every bend. Feels like a new kind of bad day. Town's wide awake now and more folks are moving along, but there are just as many stares; men in robes and turbans, women with their heads covered, kids with jars of water. The smell of bread's stronger, deceptively inviting. The move to the edge of town's easy going at first, even with the added load of money, even with the weight of stares. Hot, though, and the smell of bread starts to join with that of bodies in the heat. Round one more row to the nearest gate out but the space is open to the market stalls. Nothing for it. Time to cross.

Then they're spotted.

He's obviously a stranger, too, with a western-style hat, wide-brimmed, pulled down low. Scarf's pulled up high, so his eyes can't be seen for the shade. He's full across the market, eyes sweeping like a hawk this way and that, looking for trouble. No time for second thoughts.

Sean looks down, sees the line his foot's been drawing in the sand, looks at Emma, looks at the town, wants to leave. Emma shakes her head, grabs his hand, makes to go away. He's got to follow her.

A feeling's been on him since he got back to town, a bad feeling. Some might use the word 'ominous'. He doesn't like that feeling because that feeling says things he don't want to hear. Feelings reminding him of when he'd left on Jack's little mission. Reminding him of Walter.

It was hot as an oven without the goodness of baked things that day, just a few days ago even if it felt like forever. Sean'd just been hired. He was at the edge of town, just beyond the walls, wondering how quickly he could get back home where there're green things and trees and rivers. Then the mule showed up. He liked the mule. It was a good beast, better than all the camels he'd refused since he'd come to this place. He gave it a pat, immediately named it Walter, and looked at the boy who'd delivered him.

'From Jack,' says the little boy.

'Jack pay you for this?'

The little boy made no move one way or the other, just weighed his options and went with the safe play which was no play at all. Mighty good poker player he'd be. So Sean laughed and tossed him a coin.

'Good mule, this Amira. No mule or horse, no even camel here today.' The little boy pocketed his tip quickly.

'Really?'

'Yes. Too hot.' The little boy nodded and waved and trotted off back into town

Sean shrugged, patted the mule, said, 'Walter, how do you feel about gender-specific names?' and laughed to himself. Walter did not laugh. Too hot. In the end, it would be too hot even for poor old Walter here, but maybe Walter would have made it if Sean had stuck to the plan.

Instead he turned right from the town, east and then south and then east and then south away from the coast and the sahel, deep into the desert. Walter, or Amira, hadn't liked that much. She'd put up with it for the first two days but the two days back were harder. Nothing but sand and rocks in the desert. With a foreigner at the helm Walter was already nervous, in the end she probably knew she was doomed for she'd just stopped. Sean spurred her like the devil but she just grunted and stamped her hooves. They were at least a day from town.

So in the end Walter took the success of Sean's mission to a premature grave. Sean felt it was out of spite, for the last day of walking that brought him back to town was brutally hot and a mean wind had whipped his hat from his head. He mused briefly about the spirit of the desert. Indians back home talked that way, but he'd little reason to believe in such stuff. All he believed in then was a drink and a new mount. The latter was nowhere to be found and, now, he was worried.

Ω

'No horse, no mule,' he says to Emma. She shakes her head. Sean smacks his lips, rubs the pommel of his short blade, wishes it was a gun. A gun'd give us a chance, he thinks. The Great Equalizer'd been getting folks out of messes for a few centuries now. So he looks at Emma again, draws his index finger and thumb. 'Gun,' he says and Emma blanches. Great, he thinks, now she's upset. Dead father got it from a gun and now I've got a town full of hostiles, some strangers hunting me, *and* a worried girl to lug around—

And he's got a gun in his face. The old flintlock's in her hand, pointed at him. For a split second he thinks it's all over, that this was all some kind of ploy and now he's trapped or he's about to catch a bullet between the eyes from a child-assassin...then she lowers the gun and smirks like the little girl she is, closes up her sack. He snatches up the gun, annoyed. Guns like an antique, but beautifully kept. Some kind of old dueling pistol rich gentlemen might use when their ladies' honor had got some mud on it or the like. It's brass and wood and heavy, as much a hammer as a gun. But it feels odd, feels out of place, and, magically, it's loaded. He sticks it in his belt and whispers, 'Time to go.'

She grabs his hand, points and they scurry. They move away from the market square, but not before he catches a glance of that stranger again, who seems to sniff around for them. Something's different about him this time. Can't make it out, moving too fast through the little huts and the stares, the crunch of their feet on the sand drawing more eyes, but then they're dipping behind another house, waiting. She seems to have it down to a science, a little mouse scurrying through the living room by the best way to her hole. What he doesn't know is that she's played this game a hundred times, like she's been preparing. She's counting to ten in her mind, adds one second for good measure, then they're off again.

Her heart's pounding, thoughts moving faster than flies. She's about to leave all she knows. Just a few dozen yards and they're clear of the town's wall by the northern way, a few dozen more miles and they would reach the coast. From there, neither was sure how close they were to the nearest port.

So they're beyond the town now, no one around. Who's going to leave the shade of town? But clouds are rolling in from the west. He can't tell if that's good or bad. No matter what, it's tough by foot through the desert, even close to the sea. She's got them going due north, he's thinking northwest and tells her so. She ignores him and they keep on, trudging a ways more through the shrubs and the sand. She speeds up so he tells her again, 'This way'. She tells him what she thinks of that; a cavalcade of curses and shouts and threats. Town's still within eyeshot, maybe earshot, so he's shushing her now, wishing she'd calm down, not knowing why she's melting like this. She's shouting louder. He drops the bags, grabs her arms, and she's pounding him now, slapping at him, sobbing. He's cursing, dragging her now to a rock that just might hide them. She's collapsing, weeping.

'Jesus,' he swears, but he's got to master himself, got to get it under control and pull in the reigns. If he loses it too, then they're doomed. So he calms down, strokes her hair with shaking hand and shushes her gently. She lets him. He doesn't need to know what the episode's about, but he's got a few ideas. He thinks of a time when he was dragged away from his mother by strangers, right out of the hospital and into the street and down to the orphanage with his sister. He wanted to scream and curse then and he did and he caught it for his screaming, one slap across the face. That was the last of his screaming. He wouldn't do that to her, never would or could. She's calming down, wiping snot and tears away, muttering, 'Abbi'.

He gives her a few more minutes, got to give her that, but they have got to get away. 'Come on, girl,' he says, and hoists her up. She falls forward against him and stays there, head against his chest. He's taken aback, annoyed and on the brink of tears and wishing he was home, wishing he'd settled down long ago and had a little girl of his own. All he's got for her is a big, awkward squeeze that lasts a few seconds, then it's time to move. He doesn't know it but the squeeze let her feel the thing around his neck, the thing Jack told him to lose. They pick up their bags, he checks the gun, and the march resumes.

When the sun's high up she stops, sips some water, and puts a large scarf over her head while he wishes the brim of his hat was wider. Moving again with the sun, but the sun don't move fast enough, nor do their feet. It's all rocks and sand and dirt, but patches of crunchy grass are popping up. Thinks he can even see a hill or two with a tree on top. By day's end the terrain'll look a lot better. They stop for water often, too often he thinks, sipping then drinking greedily. Wipes his face, gets the grime out, curses his legs as they start to cramp so he drinks some more, then they resume their march.

Land's like orange couldn't make up its mind: first brown, then closer to yellow, the monochrome palette of the earth dug deep. Sun's already going down and he spies his first tree, up at the top of a big rocky knoll, a welcomed shot of green with grasping roots. That one bit of green leads to more and that's hopeful, so far as hope can go. Sun's found it's place in the low mountains to their left, amateur mountains, sun burning the sky orange. They're just about up the dry hill with the tree sticking out.

He's trying to believe the good time they've made. He's ready to collapse while this little girl's ready to keep moving, to chase those seagulls down. Twelve miles easy, he reckons. They'll hear the waves tomorrow.

He wants to make a fire but doesn't. Instead they unroll their blankets, use a little of their water supply to wash up. He's not too worried for it. Got to be water around here somewhere and they'll find it tomorrow. They eat some bread, he teaches her a few words of English. The important ones like 'eat', 'water', 'help'. Reckons there's time enough for lessons. She's his charge now, but he doesn't let that sink in. Doesn't imagine one way or the other: whether he keeps her or turns her loose, whether some uncle comes bounding up the road ready to kill him. He can't think like that. Then he hears a voice.

'Good evening.'

It's a terrible voice, like sandpaper, like a rattlesnake, and Sean sits up fast. Emma closes her eyes, heart pounding, looking for her strength. A man is squatting not three feet from them, wide-brimmed hat, scarf over his mouth, but no coat. A vest, rolled up sleeves, gun on each hip, and a curious feeling around him, like what he'd felt back in town. A dark feeling but not a terrifying one. An out-of-place feeling. Emma's mastering herself but her eyes don't open.

'Good evening,' it, or he, says again. Accent's American.

'Evening.'

'Gave us quite a chase back there.'

'Did I?'

'Yessir. Now, I've got to ask you some questions.'

Sean's a heartbeat away from drawing on him, shooting and killing him, but he waits. He's not sure why. Suddenly he wants to know this man, who's so polite, wants to hear what he has to say while resisting the urge to touch the thing around his neck.

'Why you running?'

Sean relaxes, like there's nothing to worry about, like a horrible stranger hasn't just crept upon him in the night. He licks his lips. 'Well, only two people we know in town are murdered. Seems connected.'

'Are you so sure?'

'Reckon so.'

'And you believe I'm party to that?'

'Reckon.'

'And how is that? Might be I'm just after some familiar company.'

'Can't believe you'd track us down like this if it weren't connected. Long way in the heat for an afternoon chat.' Things are making sense again, wariness and fear are coming back.

'If you had gone across the Sea or to the north of North we could track you down. It's not to do with that little town or the casualties. Well, one was a casualty, matter of safety I suppose. The other was justice. Justice is only one-half done, though. Accomplices get pulled in too, by our reckoning.'

Sean nods slowly, grips the flintlock under his blanket.

Stranger leans back, relaxes, but his voice gets deeper, more sinister like. 'Where did he have you put it, I wonder, and why? Only blood can pay for blood. Though I expect a business feller like that always sees a way out when there ain't.'

So close to drawing and shooting. He could do it too; one good shot. Done it before. But he's got to know what *it* is. So he shrugs. The stranger's eyes narrow.

'Jack's a liar. You knew that though, yeah?'

Sean shrugs again.

'Damned liar and a killer, 'long with those others he hooked into his little circle. Along with you. Feels awful close, what we're after. *Where is it?*' Stranger growls, starts to rise, hands to hips and then there's a shot and he's on his back, gurgling, dying, or so Sean hopes. The old pistol is in his hand and he looks at it and swears there's something to it, swears there's a glow, then swears it's just the brass ornaments catching the moonlight. It's quiet. Echo of the shot is long gone when she touches his arm. He starts, remembers where he is, then looks at another dead man in front of him. Stands to get a better look. His chest is red, bullet went straight through it. He twitches and stops. Hat's fallen off. His face is white, whiter than any man's could be, even if he'd been dead a minute. It's completely pale...at least on one side. The other side's all maroon, like with face paint, swirls of it loop around his eye and cheek.

Emma says something, 'Jinn', and steps back to the tree. He goes to undo the man's gunbelt but hesitates, thinking thoughts like it might burn him to the touch, like they may be cursed or the like. No use. If they're going to make it, if there's more than one of these strangers, he needs guns. Already cursed anyway. So he touches the buckle. Nothing happens. Exhales and curses himself a fool.

Undoes the belt, let's the holsters and sixguns fall away, goes to grab the man's arms to drag him down the hill but hesitates again. Nothing for it, so he grabs the man by the wrists and drags him away, Emma muttering and cursing back by the tree. Leaves the body exposed among the rocks, wonders if he'll bury it tomorrow, then he hears a scuffle and curses and wishes he'd brought the guns down. But it's not another stranger. It's a horse. It whickers in the dark, barely outlined in the moonlight. Tobiano, he thinks. He clicks his tongue, horse comes right over. Damndest thing. Horse is nuzzling the dead man, poking at his face, but his face's gone black, skin's stretching tight and crumbling.

'Now that,' says Sean, 'is the damndest thing.'

The fear's latched onto his chest like a bug, pounding

in his ears. Fear for the circle of blood, of endless retribution, of being lost and alone far from any semblance of home. Any semblance save this horse. So he grabs the animal by the bridle and rushes up the knoll to the tree and to Emma. 'We're not sleeping here,' he squeezes out between terrified breaths.

She shakes her head, sees the fear on him. Time to go, so he mounts up. Horse is kind as can be, unlike her master. Doesn't so much as grunt as he swings his leg over and sits in the saddle. Still going to have to put the beast down, he thinks, if it belonged to that stranger.

Emma's never ridden a horse before so she hesitates. She's a smart girl, though. Knows time's of the essence so she takes his offered hand, gets pulled up in front of him. But he's forgotten something: the guns. She points and says the word but all he does is stare at them. Fear's still on him, though his brain's starting to win. Knows he needs the rounds, needs the protection. That empty, old single shot on his waist won't do much when more strangers come calling. No choice.

He's off and back on in a second, guns over his shoulder, creeping up his neck like a spider. Or was it just a feeling? Without a word or a spur the horse is off, clambering up the higher side of the knoll, along the ridge and back down where it becomes a hill. Northwards. Even more grass and even less dirt now. Mountains are getting bigger on their left and the horse is looking to go around them. Sean steers her to the right, but she manages to veer to the left again, toward the foothills.

Got be late night now, he thinks. We got to rest.

But he's got another funny feeling, night's full of them. Horse knows where they're going. She'd stop as soon as he pulled the reins and called 'whoa', but she's taking them the right way. Best let it ride. So on they went, into the night, into the trees, into the grass on the hills while the dead stranger turns to dust and blows back into the desert where he came from.

6. Good Heart

Sean wakes up cold. Never got used to that, how the heat just goes away with the sun. Drops twenty degrees or more between noon and the dead of night. He's stiff as a board and groans about it to let the world know. Sleeping on the ground does that to a man. Takes his kerchief off and wipes his face, rolls over one more time and feels his loose hand touch something cold and wet. It's water, a whole lot of it. Horse took them here last night. Emma was asleep in the saddle, he barely awake, horse just plodded along and now they're here. Some small pond or other with clean water, come down off the hills and the mountains and the gulls are still there, heralds to the coming of the Sea.

Feels strange. All those years out west he never killed a man. Been in plenty of bang-ups. Maybe men died in those and he didn't know it. Shot men, but never fatal. And yet he thought when the day came, when he killed a man face to face, it would feel different. But was it a man he'd killed? He trembles, wonders how well he'll sleep not knowing if it was just the one needed killing, not knowing if he's got it in him to kill again. And then there's the horse.

Can't name the horse. Seems bad luck, and he's not sold on letting it live, so he's sticking with Horse. He dunks his kerchief in the pool and wipes his face again. Crisp and cold, enough to wake him up properly and so he rolls over and puts his face in the water, drinking up thirstily. Gets a good look at the horse and she's a beaut: tall and strong and well-kept, Appaloosa by the look of her and her coloring. Tobiano was always his favorite. Horse gazes around calmly and proudly, seeming to understand Sean's assessment of her. It's a welcome respite from shock and terror.

Emma wakes up and wants to go back to sleep. She's curled up under the blanket, got the saddle like a pillow under her little head. She's stiff, though not as stiff as Sean. Her youth's seen to that. But her brain and her heart are more worn, still raw from the last days' events. It's hard, but her youth'll see to that too, that worst of days.

'Up you go, lazy bones.' Sean's splashed a bit of water at her. She doesn't like that so she pulls the blanket over her head. 'Up you go! We missed the sunrise. Got to move, girly.'

He stands up and stretches, groaning some more, wishing he were a younger man or that, maybe, he'd taken better care of himself. Stretching and breathing relieves some of the tension, some of the fear.

The small pond is still and beautiful and there is Horse, away off to his right along the shore, grazing. They didn't bother to tether her last night; no way this horse was going anywhere. If a horse can just let a man and a girl ride it and take them all the way to safety, it could stay in one place for the night. As if she saw Emma wake up, Horse comes trotting over. Emma hears the hoofbeats and sits up. It's a kindlier wake up call than cold water. She even smiles. He hands her a water jug and a hunk of dry bread and smiles for her smile.

Horse is upon them now, pawing the ground and bobbing her head. 'She says it's time to go, too.' He looks at Emma and she understands but she waits, gets up and pats the horse's neck and says something. 'Nim,' it sounds like. Sean doesn't get it, so she puts her hand over her heart and says, 'Emma', points to Sean, 'Sean', then points to the horse. Sean shrugs and waves his hand at her. 'You pick the name'.

She thinks about it, makes sure she understands, then points to her breast.

'Chest...heart!' says Sean.

'Good Heart,' she says, for a creature must have a good heart to bear a rider like that stranger, must believe and not be afraid. Otherwise it'd kick and cry and buck. Got to have a good heart to bear bad things. Sean nods his approval and pats her head and they're up again, mounted and ready for the last stretch to the Sea.

'Alright, Good Heart. Let's go,' and they're off.

Ω

The scrub and sahel fall away quickly as they skirt the pond. Almost at once they're in a pass of some kind, dusty and grassy at the same time. Trees cause some shade, roots are sticking out like angry fingers from the overhangs. Dead end straight ahead, so they cut to the right and follow the gravelly path upwards and through.

Emma's clinging to her like a tornado's about to sweep her away, but the horse is sure-footed and strong; she's going nowhere. The path narrows and there're rock walls now, steep and narrow like a little gorge, but there's light not too far away. Wind shoots through the space like a dart and the horse picks up her pace. They're through the pass. The land is green and there's even a village off east-wards. Down through the hills, through the grass, below the gulls is the Sea.

He spurs the horse along with his heels, but Good

Heart's too smart for that; they're not yet down the gravelly, curving path that leads from the little gorge down to the coastal plain, so too much speed will send them flying. She takes it slow, easing down the slope until the green grass is under hoof, then she trots, then she canters and the rocks fly by until it's one green plain that bespeaks the promise of the Sea. She trots and the world goes away. The wind picks up and the freedom of speed overtakes them, overtakes their fears and dark strangers and the hard road before them. Fields, far away in the distance, stream by. Rivers trickle out of earshot as Good Heart breaks into a gallop. Emma giggles, leans away from Sean and waves proudly at no one, waves at the fields and the air. Grass tickles her feet. The bouncing is uncomfortable, but she doesn't really care because this is strength, this is the free air she's wished to breath though she didn't know she was wishing for it. For Sean it's only a return, a trip back home where the day to day is the sun on your back and wind in your face delivered by the wonderful beast.

The rush leaves and they get a look round. Sean does anyway, Emma's still shouting blissful things that he can't understand. She's half-weeping too. So Sean gets a good long look. Sun is at the noon. Foothills are behind them, sahel's behind that, desert is behind that. Big rock formation to the left, river beyond that, village passing by on their right; open plains before them and then, the Sea. But then what? He's gotta get his mind working, think back to his journey here, think about the one map he looked at when the boat docked and he was too anxious to pay it much heed. West makes the most sense, he thinks. West is towards civilization, east is just more desert and the world beyond. Hell, probably just as sensible to let the horse do the driving. He eases Good Heart to the left, the reins speaking his suggestion, and she follows, slowing down a bit after that burst of speed.

Emma's giggling, thinking about the wide world and the free air and the Sea. And, like that, a pack of gulls circle round to remind them of the hope ahead.

But the hope's dashed, shriveled like a fruit. Two riders are up on the ridge they'd just came down from. He can see them, dark shapes against yellow rocks catching the corner of his vision as they turn westwards. Staring across the plains, their hunting eyes must've caught them by now but there's still a chance, so long as terror doesn't stop his breath forever. Good Heart's reading his mind, galloping again toward the rocks for a bit of cover, a roll of the dice. Riders are still there, unmoving specks beyond the plain.

They dismount behind the rocks and Emma starts raving in whispers, 'Kill us!' so Sean shushes her, peeks his head up. The gaunt-men, slouched in their saddles, make for the village to the east, away from them. On the wind Sean is sure he hears a wailing shout, like a man but unlike a man. A cry of grief and woe and hatred. Good Heart grunts and twitches her ears, then paws the ground again in the shade of the rocks. Horses know. But they won't be stopping today.

Ω

The city's in view now and Emma gives a loud 'whoop!' and cries and rolls her tongue. Ride in was as beautiful as the dash from the rocks, doubly so with the sound of waves just there on the edge of hearing, the gulls a constant companion. And here's the city, their gate of salvation, and it's time to find a boat and get the hell out of Dodge.

He's not quite so optimistic. They're still pursued, still on the wrong side of the Sea, still don't know if there's a boat to be found this time of day, and he's feeling heavy.

City's a clutter of old and new buildings, mud huts and wooden four-stories, camels and horses and waggons and people brown and white, so a white man and a little brown girl stuck on a horse don't draw as many stares as they would have back in the little village on the fringe of the desert. But they still find some eyeballs on them. Tired now, burdened with fear, and saddlesore, they mean to get on a boat before the day's out. And they do.

Evening time, but the city is still alive with movement and speech. They hear at least five different languages that Sean can tell, people of all shades passing by, the meandering streets showing no sign of intention. There's a reasonable place to stop in front of a tall, western style building not far from the harbour. He tethers the horse to a bar, let's her drink up and orders Emma to the market. 'Oats,' he says. 'Hay...horse food'. Just to be sure he points to Good Heart, then points to his mouth.

She points to her mouth, pats her stomach. 'Food,' she says.

'Yeah.' He looks round. Gotta make sure no one's watching, then he walks around the horse, winces, reaches into the bag, and passes her some coin. 'Your legs aren't sore from all that riding?' She shakes her head and trots off, robe blowing in the breeze.

Looks at the horse to say, 'Guess we'll let you live,' and pats her head. Now he's got a job to do. First, got to secure things. Weapons might not be the best look for this town at this time of day, so he hides them on the saddle under some blankets; guns, blade, and all, ties them down. He's gone halfway to the first pier before it hits him: was it smart to send that girl off on her own? Strangers everywhere, and not all of them the ghoulish sort. So he heads back.

[44]

There are snakes at every turn and bad stares behind him. The dirt paths intersect and crisscross in seeming disorder. He knows the way. A few turns and he can see Good Heart down the road, still lapping water placidly. But there are two legs between her four, hands groping at her saddle, so he starts to run and sees the feet are sandled, the hands small. It's Emma, safe and victorious. Hay's stacked high in front of the horse. Still, better to keep her close. He whistles and waves and she trots over to him, tired but smiling.

Daylight is creeping away like a thief so they move quick down to the harbor. She points back to Good Heart, 'Ok?'

'Yeah, she'll be okay. Folks round here obey the law, far as I can tell. That horse can take better care of herself than either of us can anyways.'

The harbor is much bigger than he remembers. About a dozen piers line the coast, wooden boardwalks, and ships. Lots of ships. One of them's got to be making a night voyage. So they keep moving, trying to find someone who looks like a captain. He hears some men standing around, speaking a language he can understand. He butts in.

'Tiene nave? Ir alli?'

They stop their talk, look annoyed and shake their heads. Emma's asking now, in her tongue. She mostly gets bad looks and soon it's more than that. One of the two takes the pipe he'd been smoking out of his mouth and grants a few choice words in Spanish, words Sean doesn't quite know but the tone grants enough understanding. Fingers the thing around his neck before speaking.

'Say, I don't care for all that,' says he.

The one rolls his eyes and mutters something else and Sean is sure he's caught 'cabrón' coming out of his mouth. Anyone spent any time near any Spanish knows that one.

So he stands up taller, leans in, 'Reckon where I come from a man get flayed talking like that. Now why don't you jog on before I find me a whip. *Fuera!*'

Man shakes his head again, walks away slowly, smoke streaming from his head as he goes.

Emma raises her eyebrows to Sean's smug satisfaction.

'What?' he asks innocently.

☊

Somewheres along the way the asking comes to them. Perhaps the commotion spread the word on their behalf. Sun's just about down when someone calls her over. Calls her 'little girl', but she don't mind. He's ugly. Looks like a meatball with a beard, she thinks, but he's claiming to have a boat. She tells him what they want, ignores the awkward, indecent leer the sailor behind him passes her way. Gotta conjure up some English for her friend now, so she says, 'Morning.'

Sean's got his hands on his hips, not liking this fellow. Probably a dirty fisherman looking to take advantage and make some easy money. 'No,' he says. 'Tonight or not at all.' Points downwards. 'Tonight.'

Meatball's laughing now, gesturing his hand in the international sign for money, running his mouth some more. Emma thinks she could shoot the man then and there for the dirty things he says, what he suggests about her and her new friend. Even if she could find the words, she would not tell Sean. She knows they need to go. Maybe the strangers will come back one day and punish this man for his rotten mouth.

Sean starts tossing coins at meatball who manages to catch them with a little struggle, then he holds up his hands and yells something so Sean stops.

'More,' she says.

Sean pauses, thinks, doesn't like what he's thinking then says, 'Alright.'

7. THE SEA

Meatball likes the sixgun. They hadn't got a good look at it in their escape, but it's nice. Real nice. The grip's woven with something that looks like gold, metal is all black matte with more gold wound round the barrel. It's not loaded. The fat man rotates it in his hand, looks down the sights like he knows what he's doing. He doesn't. He's muttering and smiling and Emma looks like she'd give anything to punch him in his eye. Sean's dead tired and needs this ship to sail and quickly so he nudges Emma and she asks.

Meatball nods and says something to the other man who's there in his quarters, the dingy little room the captain keeps for himself. The man leaves, heads back above deck. Sean pulls the old flintlock, Emma's dueling pistol, out of his belt and holsters it in the now empty spot on his hip. The left. The right holster's got the brother to the gun he just sold to get them across the Sea. He's not happy about it but they have got to go. He's thinking of pale white faces turning black and blowing away, but not before those faces have hands and the hands have guns and the guns have bullets to put between his eyes.

Captain Meatball's speaking again. Sean wishes he wouldn't. He points at the dueling pistol and Sean immediately, instinctively puts his hand on it. 'Not for sale,' he says. 'Not — for — sale.'

Meatball holds up his hands in a sign of peace but his

smirk belies its sincerity. Sean ignores it. Can't get a man like that to listen to reason anyhow. Got to show it. He can feel the ship moving a bit, hears the calls above deck. Captain Meatball gets up, bids them follow and shows them to the tiny cabin that's theirs. One small bed and a bare floor. He smiles like a devil and walks away.

Door's shut now. Emma's about asleep as she stands. He gestures to the bed. 'Get some sleep. I'm gonna go check on Good Heart.' She nods and gets into the bed without question. Down the corridor now. Ship's big, but not too big. Big enough to hold a bunch of fish and smells like it, too. He hopes the captain understands where they're meant to go and that there's to be no trouble. No time to wish for a pleasure cruise, he thinks. Good Heart's in a big hold that smells even more of fish. She's agitated, sweating a bit and dancing anxiously here and there. But the Sea's calm and the horse is getting used to the motion. He throws down more hay and puts bails for her to lean against if she can rest. He's not expecting she will. Pats her anyway, whispers nice things that horses like to hear, wonders if she understands English. Wonders what language the strangers speak. He promises to come back shortly.

Got to get away from that fishy smell, so he goes up on deck. They haven't got as far as he hoped or thought. The city and the harbor are still there, not too far away. Wind's come in, blowing the clouds away and bringing a beautiful clear night. He wants to see the stars out at Sea, but doubts he'll stay awake for them. Looks back at the city. Faint lights are still up and the moon provides a spotlight.

His heart catches, stops, then beats again because he's sure he can see it, an outline of two figures with wide hats at the tip of the longest pier staring out at the Sea.

Staring at him. One of them waves merrily. He thinks that's enough air for now.

Back below deck he's got to pass by their room before getting back to Good Heart and there's someone at their door, kneeling down and listening. It's the first mate. His soft boots don't make much sound so Sean paces forward. First Mate's head is turned away, got his ear on the door and now the rage is building in Sean like a gale. He doesn't like being spooked, as he'd been up on deck, and he doesn't like men who snoop on little girls. Pulls out the flintlock, holds it by the barrel, screws up his face and swings, shouting 'Bastard!' He's so mad that the pistol whip goes wide, grazing his head and cuffing his ear more than anything, but the man whimpers and goes down all the same, scurrying on all fours away from Sean like a rat.

Sean kicks him in the ass and he falls on his face and gasps and keeps crawling. Sean thinks he ought to beat him, break a few ribs to teach him a lesson, but it's probably not worth it. Not worth getting dumped into the Sea by a meatball and leaving Emma here alone. So he lets the snoop alone, creeps inside their cabin and sits on the floor, goes to speak to Emma but she's sprawled on the small bed, a blanket dangling on her leg there in the dark; she's slept through the whole thing.

Sean draws his gun for the first time, the second black pistol he took from the dead man. It feels odd in his hand and he can't decide if it's because it's the gun of a dead man or if it's just a new gun. Either way, it'll shoot whoever comes through that door. Admiring the thing, he wills himself not to think too much, not care that it feels the same as the flintlock, like the guns are related. He leans against the cabin wall and waits.

Next day, up on deck and they're surrounded by nothing but the wine-dark Sea. Emma'd woken him up just as light was trickling through the roof of their cabin. No more trouble in the night. And most of the crew's taken kindly to Emma, in spite of the demands of maritime superstition. Only ones seem to avoid her are the captain and first mate, but at least the captain will crack a smile when she passes. Sean gives the first mate a dirty look each chance he gets. Crew don't seem to mind the break from hauling fish all day; Captain must have been generous with spreading Sean's absurd payment around. Ship's got no galley so they munch on crusty bread and salted fish. Probably all they'll get to eat until dinner, but there're still some provisions in their cabin. Doesn't matter. This time tomorrow they'll feel the earth under their heels.

The call was tough; take the longer road and get closer to where Sean wanted to go, or the shorter and get Good Heart back on land as quick as can be, running the risk of open travel. In the end they'd split the difference, through Sean's request and Emma's poor translating. That meant this second day at sea and this day would be among the most dull Sean or Emma'd ever had.

Come afternoon, when the sun was less a burden and he finally felt comfortable enough to leave Emma be, he went back below deck to see Good Heart again. The horse is a wonder, he thought. She champed thoughtfully on what was left of the hay and oats and seemed happy, happy as a horse could be while cooped up in a boat, though the hold was spacious enough. He'd dealt with a lot of horses in his time, breaking and riding, and most were kindly creatures, but fickle. This one's like a saint. Patient. He's got no brush. Rubs his hands along her, pats her, scratches her, makes her feel comfortable. Notes a few hurts and discolorations on her back from the ride, but no sores. Before he'd been a package for this ferrier, now he wants to be the rider, the master. Scratches her mane then he reveals the grand finale; a small, dried apple he'd bought in town and hung on to. Shoves it in her mouth and she chomps gratefully, twirling it with her tongue to get all the flesh off. He's feeling satisfied, pats Good Heart with the briefest of smiles.

'Wasn't always I knew the way around horses,' he began. 'Started off finding whatever work I could to survive, here and there all up around Oklahoma, Nebraska. Time's was lawless when I was a boy after the War. Got good enough to shoot, better with horses. Figured I could do that everywhere, everywhere as folk rode horses. Reckon they won't be replaced any time soon even with those giant steam engines. Ain't too many of those in Spain, 'specially in the south. Still horse country there. Still like back home. Prettier, though.'

Horse's as fine and polite a listener as he could want. Regards him thoughtfully. He allows himself a wistful smile, pats Good Heart once more, but a darkness interrupts the moment. Can't shake the feeling of seeing two strangers last night. Too eerie and upsetting to think on in full. Can't say if they'll follow or if that was a wave g'bye or if they were even connected. Either way, he'll stay ready. Ready for the rest of his days, need be. Ready for however many of them come looking. But looking for what?

The trinket.

The thought strikes like lightning. They're after Jack's little trinket, that medal he was sent to lose. Guess I already knew that, he thinks. Didn't care to hold on to the thought, but there it is.

Reasoning doesn't sit quite right with him, though,

about the trinket. He's tapping it lightly, through his shirt.

'Can't be worth keeping if it's this much trouble,' he says. 'Got me enough money for the present, anyhow.'

Good Heart gives him a look he thinks he can almost understand. Says to her 'You'll be talking before too long,' and then he's off again.

Can't say where to. Indecision gets him back on deck to find Emma playing some kind of dice game or other with the sailors. He feels like he could use a nap but he also feels there'll be time for napping when they're away from this rowdy bunch, on land and under something shady. Pinto horses come to mind, dirt and sand and shady palm trees and Abel with his dirty jokes and a nice meal waiting at the end of every day. Thinks of wine and civilized places where a man rides all day and his work is welcomed. Thinks of running errands for a thief out in the desert and thinks he's glad to be getting away from there, even glad to be at Sea. Not a month of that mess and he's glad Jack is out of his life...not glad he's dead, though.

♎

Day's passing like a turtle. Emma, who'd just gotten used to being the kid sister of the crew, is already bored. Sun's in the west so they're getting there, but they really want to be there already. Good Heart's a trooper, uncomplaining, while the other two of their party mope about on deck, catching glimpses of land here and there and then seeing their hope drift away. Sean's thinking of sleep, but he's also thinking that he wants an eye on Emma. He sits her down, teaches her some more English, just random words he thinks of as they're sitting there, rolling with the Sea.

'Man,' he says and points to himself.

Emma nods. 'Men,' she says unintentionally.

'Good enough. Hair.' Points to his hair. 'Brown hair.'
Emma nods again.

He looks over starboard. 'Water.'

She nods.

'Are you getting any of this?'

Blank stare. She gives it a moment then takes a risk.
'Yes?'

Sean smiles. 'Good!'

This keeps on for a while, Sean being a patient teacher.
Easier to teach clever girls than horses, he thinks. And so
he does. Seems she'd already had a start before he'd even
met her. They go from 'water' to 'sea' to 'ocean' before he
realizes synonyms aren't worth the time. 'Fat' he says as the
Captain passes by. Emma nods seriously. Sean laughs and
gives her a squeeze on the wrist she doesn't understand,
but accepts. Her father was not an affectionate man, so
it's a welcomed thing. Puts her off nonetheless.

Now she's trying not to think of her father, just wants
to learn more English and make Sean happy. Just wants
to get off this boat and find a new place to live, with or
without Sean. Hopefully with him.

Ω

Night time now and they're in the same positions in the
cabin. Sean's leaning against the wall, hat on the floor,
wishing for a bath while Emma snores loudly on the small
bed. Eyes are heavy, can't think anymore or see straight.
Time to sleep and be ready to disembark in the morning.
He'd checked on Good Heart once more and the wonder
beast was the same; patiently, calmly eating and moving
about the hold, or laying down and resting against the
stacks of hay. Now it's his turn to rest.

Not all men are interested in rest, though. That first

mate isn't. He's got things on his mind, dark things and he's not sure where they came from. Scares him. Scares him more to resist. They told him what to do, how to do it, and how much they'd pay him to do so. Now the job's to be done.

Door doesn't creak when he enters, neither do his feet. Even his blade is silent, that short, sharp dagger. Two strides and he's at Emma's bed, one hand's on the blade the other goes for her hair. He yanks, she squeals and Sean is on him a second later and they're tumbling to the ground. It's a bad sound, a box full of grunts and shouts and a little girl screaming and stamping. Now Sean screams and the blade hits the ground. Got him in the side, but now he's on top. First Mate's on his back, Emma's on top of him and Sean's on top of her. He's got one hand on Sean's throat, weak grip, the other's on Emma's throat, strong grip getting stronger. Sean's right is trying to free her, the left is holding him up.

There are no words, only a struggling scuffle and growls. And then it slips out, as if bidden. Dangling around Sean's neck, the trinket sways. It's gold, ornate, and wondrous. Moment slows, the first mate eyeing the prize, Sean feeling it pull on his neck. Then time returns. Emma turns red as a beet. Sean can't get the grip loose and there's a rage in him like he's never known.

'You go to hell!' and he jabs his thumb in the first mate's eye. Poor soul howls but he lets go and they all collapse to the floor and Sean feels sick. Main thing is Emma's breathing. Breathing and crying. Sean shudders, thinking of a thumb in his eye, shudders again for rage and sets Emma on the bed. Now he strides back over to the assailant. His boots are soft but they still hurt when he stamps First Mate between his legs. Stamps three times and wonders if the first mate is going to throw up. He doesn't.

Girl's just plain crying now, no struggle to breath. She's scared, scared and angry. Angry for being weak again and for this man surprising her and for Sean letting it happen. She notices the thing just before Sean tucks it back into his shirt. Sputters a few choice words in her first language, then a few more in English, then Sean is there rubbing her back and she starts to calm down just in time for the cavalry to pull up.

Captain Fat Man Meatball leads the charge but it's two crewmen who pick First Mate up. Blood's on the hand that covered his eyes and the lids are swollen to hell but the eye is still there. Sean feels his dinner coming back up at the thought of seeing an eyeball hanging down but there's not one. Emma screams at the captain in their language. He nods solemnly and fingers the gun on his hip.

Ω

Alone now. She's laying on the tiny bed, shuddering, and he sits erect doing his damndest to calm the room and calm it gets. Quiet relief is among them, a certain security between the pair. If bonds can be made in short time, if they hadn't already been made between this man and this girl on the long road from the desert, they're made then and made the stronger. They let the silent understanding sit between them and minister to them and they rest, almost comfortably.

By the time they both calm down and get on deck for some air, First Mate is blindfolded and leaning on the railing of the forecastle deck. One of the crewman is saying a prayer. They all look solemn and the first mate starts crying like he's a kid wishing to wake up from a nightmare.

'Now wait just a minute.'

First Mate manages a few words between sobs and the Captain shakes his head and Sean hears it again, 'Insha'Allah', and there's a gunshot and the first mate tips over the railing and into the wine-dark sea. Emma jumps at the shot and looks more ragged than ever. Sean swears the pistol shimmers before the captain holsters it again.

He wants off the ship as bad as she does, if not more because he wants it for Emma too, to be on dry land where he can protect her and where the bad men are easier to run from and no eyes need plucking out. But there is no off, no safe place for a few more hours at least, if there are any safe places left in the world. They sit on the deck and he puts his arm around her and she falls asleep in his arms and he feels awkward, this being out in the open. The awkwardness goes away after a while and suddenly it's nice. Suddenly he's back in that quiet surety, a father, and he's under the stars with his daughter asleep in his arms, not a girl he's only known for days and can scarcely understand.

Lays her down gently and stands, facing the black wall of night. Almost without thought he takes it off, holds it in his hands, notes its weight. What was I thinking? he wonders. Though it calls him, though it's intriguing, it's dirty. Dirty money, covered in blood. Not worth the trouble it's brought to him and Jack and Emma, to First Mate, and whoever else it may touch. Time to do what he was paid to. Exhales and launches the pendant into the blackness. Doesn't hear it plunk, doesn't watch it go. He sits back down next to Emma and decides to move on.

The lurching of the Sea is their mother rocking them to sleep. None of the crew bother them because they're a decent enough bunch and they know these two have had enough for one day and they can sleep on deck if they want.

Sean dozes.

The edge of his sleep is encrusted with bad dreams of bad men coming after him until Good Heart arrives on hooves of flaming thunder. She keeps on galloping away, over the Sea, and the flames on her feet burn his old house down, burn down the orphanage he knew and the town, wherever it was, in which his sister lived. And when those things blew down and he knew he was asleep it was quiet and dark and warm and there were no bad men. Just his mother rocking him to sleep.

8. Bibiana

She wakes up to the sound of gulls and her father smiling down at her. But it's not her father. It's Sean. This odd foreigner who loves her so much. I must love him, too, she thinks.

Stiff, she wishes she had a blanket to pull over her head, a pillow to roll over on. All she's got is a splintery, wooden deck. And Sean. And Good Heart. Her frown breaks at that, turns around and she wishes they were stopped so she could ride Good Heart again, away from prying pirates and evil men to a little house somewhere in green lands with green grass. He lifts her to her feet, under her arms, and her wish comes true; boat's stopped and they're looking over the prow of the ship to land, to a town, tan and wonderful with arches and shingled roofs. Nice enough. Nicer than a bunch of mud huts out at the edge of the desert, anyhow.

He's had time to go over the nights events and think on them and no answers came. Can't help but to know it's connected with the strangers, with Jack, Emma's father, with this whole conspiracy he's embroiled in and does not understand. As they dock the choice is before him: dwell on it, or keep moving, and he chooses the latter, just as he always does; leastways he must, as the sea-voyage is at an end. This time, thought, the moving's got to end. Time to settle and put down roots, time to find a fort to defend, their very own Alamo if it must be.

Looks like the crew were ready to get past this journey, too, because they're already off, eager to spend their pay on something to make them forget the trouble of the night before. Good Heart's down there, champing and stomping, tied to a post away from the berth. Gulls are still there, chirping their song, the song of children who love to sing but can't do it well. Wind and waves are the backing band, but the moment don't last.

She feels disgusting and exhausted, like she's been through the wringer and she has; no bath in days, life on horseback, terror in the night. Looks at Sean, sees he's letting the moment sweep him up, staying in the right now; refusing to go back to night-shadows. Might be she could do that, too. Pretty enough day for it, anyhow.

Looks down at her with that ridiculous hat still on. Says, 'Ready, girl?' She thinks she knows what he means and nods and takes his outstretched hand. Down the gangplank and across the berth to the quay and men are already speaking a new language. Doesn't sound too different from hers, but they use their tongues a lot more than their throats. And why shouldn't they? The little bit of land she can see, the dirty green hills rising beyond the town, roll like the language, roll like the Sea. Not like the choppy water, choppy sand and ridges that birthed her speech. But that was far away, farther than her little town across the Sea, and it didn't matter right now. Good Heart's here. That splotchy hide, though still lovely, was a little worse for two days cramped up in a fish hold. She looks dirty and it makes Sean mad but then again they're all dirty. Pats the horse, looks around, smiles at Emma, wants to believe they're as safe as they are dirty.

'You need a bath, little girl.'

Blank stare. So he sniffs himself and makes a face like sour cheese. She laughs and says, 'Dirty'.

'Yeah. Dirty.'

$$\Omega$$

Town's not much cleaner but the arches and spackle make it look beautiful and ancient. Emma sees things that look like they belong far away, in the desert: curves and script and tiles. Early yet so it's not too busy, but stalls fill up. Bread is baking, tea is brewing. Fish are everywhere. The shade of the buildings is almost too cool but they both know to enjoy it because even the sea-breeze won't keep the heat out come midday.

'Establo? Caballeriza?' He's asking just about everyone. Emma guides Good Heart and the beast seems every inch as interested in this new place as she is. Eyes take everything in with quiet, human patience. Folks are brown. Not quite as brown as the desert, but brown. Dress is different, too, and the language and the food and the smells. It's a halfway point, though, the gray between the black and white of different worlds with the Sea being the middle of that line.

He keeps asking, figures there's at least one decent human being in this town, figures not everyone is put out seeing a man with guns on his hips. Emma taps his shoulder and he turns and at once he sees two men halfway down the alley behind them. Two fishermen from the ship, Captain Meatball's men, staring right at him. But he's got a taker now and can't afford them any heed. A little boy, younger than Emma, tugs his sleeve and says something about a stable. Sean slips him a coin and they follow him and he turns this way and that, minutes upon minutes, to the edge of town where the smells are lighter and the buildings thinner. Every other step Sean's turning, praying not to see the two fishermen. Can't tell if they're after them or just in the wrong place at the right time. Soon the town is a bit behind them, and to his left he makes out sheer rocks along the coast, dropping down silently to the Sea. By the time the buildings thin out behind them he sees no one, prays it stays that way.

The stable is a small, low building with a shabby man sleeping outside. Got the largest white sideburns anyone had ever seen. Sways in his chair and the boy throws something at him. Rock pings on the porch and he jolts up with a start, curses the boy who runs away waving. Sean waves now, speaks to Sideburns in his tongue, or tries to anyway. Sideburns gets it, smiles at the horse and girl and gestures inside. Sean tells him no and they lead Good Heart around back, to the stall. Stall's clean, if not perfect: slats in the door, fresh hay, window, cool and shady and right. Sean nods and gives Sideburns some coins and slaps a brush in his hands, pats him on the shoulder.

'No, no,' he says. 'Café primero!' and puts the brush back. Coffee first. Smiles, bows low and gestures for Good Heart to enter the stall.

'No.' Sean leads them back outside. There's a double paddock and he lets Good Heart in of his own accord. Sideburns don't mind one bit. Horse likes it, too, starts prancing around the yard, shaking her mane and neighing. It's a good sight.

Coffee's not bad either. Emma's in the chair on the porch. The two men stand. Sean sips his coffee, held in his right hand, left is in his pocket, one leg propped up on the porch and he leans into it and suddenly Emma sees him in his element. He's at home here, even exhausted, even with the wrong kind of hat and the wrong kind of gun in one holster. This is where he's supposed to be, though she doesn't really understand the feeling. Feels like he is lodged here in this moment.

He drinks the rest of the coffee down, slings their things over his shoulder, says, 'Let's go' and Emma follows. Lets Sideburns know they'll be back soon and already she's tugging on his arm. He likes it, likes feeling annoyed and having this kid to tend to in the clear morning after a cup of coffee and hopes she likes it too.

'To church!' he declares. She doesn't know what that means.

Ω

What it means is sanctuary, and a clean place to rest. She thinks it means a palace of idols. Doesn't understand the iconography, all the pictures and crosses. To make matters worse there's a storm brewing outside. God is angry. Before the first plinks of rain struck the roof of the church they'd stepped into the empty foyer and he crossed himself instinctively. Not even Catholic, he thought.

Emma'd just looked at him like he was crazy and he dragged her through the foyer and over to the pews and they'd set their things down and waited. Finally a priest came out from the back and now they're here, waiting, two foreigners, one of them a little girl from the desert, the other a tall American.

Sean wipes his nose nervously. 'Gracias, padre.'

The priest nods and looks nervous as the last word echoes through the empty place, off the saints and the confessional and the altar. It's a beautiful church, but simple. All adobe with wood furnishings. Small statues of saints probably crafted locally. Polished wood altar preceding a large cross. Chapels on either side of the altar closed off by homespun curtains. Sean takes it in, sweats a little more, and tries to explain. Tells him that he's looking after this girl, that her father is dead, that they've got no place to go. Why not the hostel in town? The inn? Sean stares for a minute, his eyes wide, the creases in the corners more visible than ever. Then he shakes his head and leaves it at that but he's thinking about strangers, about a grown man going into a hotel with a girl. Got to be safer here, at least for one night, and before he can figure out how to say what he's thinking in Spanish that look crosses priests' face. That piteous look that befits a priest's title: *father*.

He's a gray man who keeps his beard short. Handsome, much handsomer in is his youth no doubt, but one of them blessed old men who's managed to keep his shape. No gut or neck-meat. Must do some heavy lifting here and there, Sean thinks, then comes the image of a young man robbed by love who goes to the Church for recompense. What he's got is a lifetime of service and, most probably, the love of God. Could be true, could be his story. Could easily have been Sean's story as that kind of thing appealed to Sean, once. But his God, probably the same God in fact, lives out amongst the stars and between the brush and the dirt and the grass and over a horse.

Don't matter, though. They've come to him and they're at his mercy and he grants it and he looks at Emma and Sean thinks the old priest is going to cry. Sees hurt there and brokenness and he nods again and puts his hand on her shoulder and mutters something in his language. A hard clink comes from one of the little chapels and breaks the moment. Sean thinks he hears a curse; odd place for it, too.

She emerges from behind the curtain under a black shawl, lovely tan face peeks out but it's turning red, redder for three pairs of eyes on her. Won't even glance their way, just heads for the door as the crow flies. Rounding the pews, she manages to look up at Sean and they both stop and take each other in. A second later she's moving again and he thinks he just took one to the gut, like her gaze cost him a rib or two. Emma notices.

'Bibiana.' The woman stops like a stone. Priest waves her over. 'Ven aqui.'

She won't turn so quick. Priest says her name again and this time she turns round, but slow. Can't say why. Maybe she's embarrassed. Maybe just scared or maybe she just wants to get home for dinner. Either way, she obeys Priest. There's a respect there, or so Emma deems. This woman isn't just loyal to her church, afraid for God to smash her if she disobeys; there's respect, or at least softness, for the man. Sean just looks foolish, like a mule someone's asked to do accounts.

Priest speaks again. 'Bibiana. Él es americano. Por favor, ayúdame con el Inglés.'

Again she hesitates. Her face is blank, mouth set until it opens. Sean thinks it's the voice of an angel-bird, the tweet of the heavens. 'Why are you come here?'

His turn to play the part of the mute. His mouth moves but nothing comes out and of a sudden he's very self-conscious of his appearance, his shabby beard, his stench, and the fact that he's wearing a gun in church.

'Is the father wrong?' she asks, 'Do you not speak English?'

'No.' Hands on his hips now. Got to look at the floor to maintain. 'No. I mean, yes. I speak English. Little Spanish, too, but not enough for padre here.' Emma watches them with hawkish eyes, albeit the heavy eyes of a hawk fighting sleep. 'We, ehm...I can't think of no place else for us to hold up. We need to get cleaned, some place safe to sleep. Food. I can pay...' Thinks of a church far away, of a moustachioed preacher. 'Or, make a sizable donation to the church.'

'Go to the inn. There are two in town.' Her voice is hard, but not steel. More like compacted earth.

'No,' says Priest. Guess he understands that much English. He shakes his head to show he means business.

While Priest explains himself, Sean takes her in once more. Not much of a story to tell in her long, black dress, mantle, and gray scarf, but her face radiates like a candle in the dim church. High cheekbones, full lips, thin, black eyebrows. Man can't think of another woman's he's seen who casts this spell. She's saying something, something lovely and important.

'How's that?' He slowly gets back to the moment.

'I ask you what happened. To you and the girl.'

Sean's not eager to recount the story, waits and lets his brain bone out the details. Sniffs. 'I was working across the Sea. In the desert there. I found her alone, her father dead next to her. The men as killed him, or I believe killed him, killed a friend of mine too. And were looking for us next day. So we ran. Here we are.'

Emma's still. Sits on the pew with her knees drawn and a hand in her hair, bags under her eyes telling the story of her fatigue. Almost nods off a couple times and looks piteous. Also looks like she'd chew your pity up and spit it out at your feet.

'And this girl has no family?'

'Far as I know.'

The woman looks dubious. 'And why *here*? Why not back home?'

'Ma'am, this place's much home as home is. Been working here for about three years now—'

'And your Spanish is still so bad?'

Sean laughs, she doesn't. 'Ehm...back home I knowed Mexicans lived stateside for half their lives, can't so much as ask for coffee.' She doesn't accept the reasoning, apparently, so Sean gets serious. Reckons an honest appeal might be best. Days of feeling gush out. He'd taken no time to think about it, to let things settle in, and he hates it but out it comes. 'I have no plan, ma'am. I have this girl in my charge and I don't know what to do. I don't even know if she's only with me because she's too scared to leave, or if she *wants* to be with me and if I stop and let myself feel what needs feeling then the walls start closing in.' Waves a hand vaguely. 'Forms come out of the shadows. I'm ragged. All I've got is this dirty getup you see, Emma,' he nods her way, 'a horse, and some money. I'm a man without work, without time, and all I want is some damned sleep.'

The last word is choked and he looks down again. He blushes, waves his apology to the priest who probably couldn't tell he'd just profaned in God's house. The woman nods slowly, mouth still set, but her eyes are open. Her face shows she believes him. Holds out her hand. 'Bibiana Varela.' He takes it, grins his relief, grins to touch so fine a hand. He sniffs and gracefully wipes a tear and says, 'Sean Denman. How do you do.'

'Well.' She claps her hands. 'We shall get you cleaned up, Mr. Denman, for you smell like that horse you mentioned earlier. And fish.'

He laughs a freer laugh than he's had in weeks. A few jokes about her washing him come to mind but he holds back. Been too long since he's been around a proper lady and he don't want to mess it up just yet.

Not ever, he thinks.

She sings softly in a language Emma can't understand. Catches a few words here and there, but it's like trying to remember a dream. Makes her tired and she's too tired already. Sean had asked her to do it. Much as he likes thinking of this little desert girl as his daughter he's not ready to help her bathe, too grown for it anyway, and she didn't want to be alone. So it fell to Bibiana. Emma fought it at first. There was no tub at the church, no proper place for a girl to wash or be washed, just a stall the priest used next to his quarters and that was for Sean. She wouldn't be parted from him and made it very clear until Sean grabbed her by the shoulders, said his soothing words and made her look at Bibiana. No, she didn't seem like someone who meant her harm. Besides, her house was just across the street from the church and he'd come and see her just as soon as she was done. She nodded like she understood, and she did.

Once they'd crossed the street, having looked and looked again for any strangeness, and gone into the house, she'd taken off her scarf and Emma saw that her face was very kind. But even the most kindly-faced women could be devils. Bibiana felt nothing like one. She's very gentle and Emma knows she shares her sense of loss somehow. Her house was kindly as well.

It was only of two rooms: the sitting room with a small kitchen attached and the bedroom, which also contained the bath. It was small but warm, the first western-style home Emma'd seen. She thought the curtains too much, a waste of cloth, but the rest she liked, felt herself get comfortable even. Sun went down and they'd had a light dinner of soup and flatbread. The girl had sopped it up greedily, having no real manners and starving. She tried to let herself feel safe and enjoy her full stomach, but she swore she heard footsteps on the floorboard and thought of strange men at the door.

Modest as she was, Emma had felt no shame in stripping down in her presence. Bibiana had been decent enough to turn aside, but Emma would not have cared either way. The fear'd gone, though it lingered at the edge, and a safety she did not and does not understand took its place, the same way she felt when Sean had found her.

Now she's in this tub of water and the water's too hot. She thinks of all the times her father'd told her about hell. But here things are clean and sweet smelling and hot water isn't enough to convince her that hell is just around the corner. Bibiana scrubs her back methodically, singing like a timid starling all the while. Emma slips in and out of sleep, drawn back by the song and the restful presence of this woman, letting the strangers in her imagination flit away round darkened corners.

Bibiana pats the girl on the head. 'Up you get, sleepy bug.'

She gets up and wonders what *bug* means, wraps herself in the offered towel and shakes her head groggily, hoping to dash the sleepiness against the walls of her mind so she doesn't trip and fall out of the slippery tub. The candles make for calm light and that don't help. Rest of the room is simple but feminine. Like a very grown up girl's room: delicate figures placed here and there atop a nicely carved dresser. Four-post bed, wooden armoire, a little altar on her nightstand and one crucifix on the back of her door. Emma doesn't like the crucifix. Why have dead men in your room?

'I will wash your clothes tomorrow. You can wear this for now.' She hands her a nightgown. It's frilly and Emma hates frills. She'd rather have simple cotton cloth but she can't explain that and would be rude to anyway. So she takes it, puts it on, and feels like some stupid Pasha's daughter for a moment. But it is nice and soft. And clean. 'I'll bother about the tub in the morning as well. I think we're both too tired for all of that. I always read before rest, but let us say our evening prayers so that you can sleep.'

She's kneeling now, motioning for Emma to join her by the bed. This Emma knows, but when the woman folds her hands and closes her eyes it becomes foreign. Folds her hands anyway, not sure of what else to do. Seems right in its way, if odd, and the woman's kindly and is sharing her soft bed with her. It must be soft, like a pit of feathers, so much nicer than the cot on the ship, even softer than her own bed. But the time's for praying so she kneels and folds her hands and the woman speaks, saying, 'Te Deum laudamus: te Dominum confitemur...' Discomfort sweeps over the girl and she wonders if God is displeased with these prayers. Her father had been religious, in his way, but they did not attend prayer regularly and rarely read scripture. She can still remember the caller, though, and how her father stopped to pray each time...well, almost every time. Bibiana comes to a close, 'Amen', and Emma decides God can't mind too much. Better to believe and to pray, even in the wrong way, than to ignore Him. The thought sticks with her though, and as she curls up in the bed, soft covers enveloping her like a womb, and she wonders where God is and what He is doing. If He is with the Priest or with Sean, if He's angry at the strangers who killed her father and if His justice will be swift in coming.

Thoughts get muddy, stick together, ball up and become dreams. Sounds reach her. Sounds of boots on floorboards and the shifting of curtains as Bibiana drops the book and goes to the window. Hears the woman hiss and shut the curtains and go into the other room and then she sleeps, glad that the world has gone away for a while.

Ω

Priest speaks too fast for Sean's addled mind to translate. Being a good priest, the man keeps wine in his quarters and now he's sharing it with the foreigner. Really, the man's glad for the company. The solitary life gets lonesome; even with Christ and His saints and his flock a little company at night is welcome. Still gauging the foreigner, thinking he wants to trust him but he can't just yet. Meanwhile Sean's thinking he's a sucker for the taste; wine's going to put him to sleep before he can clean up and check on Emma. And Bibiana. Guns are resting by his feet, against the legs of the chair here in the tiny room. Like a closet with a bed and a desk, really, but better than out there on the street or at a guest house. Better than that ship. Hats off, dangling on a peg in the wall, but his boots are on. Won't go and see the girls barefoot.

Priest is going on about something. Something about the females being separate and that it was a good thing. Now he's saying something about the Lord and the stars. Is he praying? No. Probably just getting drunk. Mutters 'Bibiana' and shakes his head. Sean's interested now.

'¿Conoce Bibiana?'

'Si, si...' Priest goes on rapid fire but Sean picks most of it up. He's laughing while he talks, like he's reminiscing about his child. Might as well have been. Woman grew up in this town, in this church. Knew the priest from birth, practically; he's the one baptised her. Religious family, well-to-do. Had a nice ranch on the outskirts of town where they kept horses and cows and sheep, mostly for the pleasure and the fresh meat and cheese. Father made good money teaching English at a small school and offered private lessons to the many trading families that lived in town. Bibiana was their only child. Mother hated it, thought a woman ought to have a flock of kids hiding under her skirts. A real woman would raise an army of little people to march in formation and dance on command, but she just had Bibiana. Priest thought she tried to hide those feelings from the girl, but it got through anyway. Bibiana'd never been close to her mother, in tight with her father, though. Both of them were dead now. Father went on years earlier, mom just after her wedding so more's the pity.

'Wait, wait. Wedding? ¿Ella tiene esposo?'

Priest goes dark at that, peers into his cup frowning. Bibiana's husband is dead, too. Murdered three years earlier. Only been married a year, too. Bibiana'd practically lived at the church after that. Wore black for six months straight. Husband was a good man, a teacher like her father who loved animals, coffee, and vacationing. Their honeymoon had been a cruise upon the Sea, stopping here and there to see who else lived along that glorious ocean. Turned out they liked it here best; near the Sea and near to home. Near to church, too. Husband was from the big city, but he liked small town living. Quiet enough, if not a little dirty. Plenty of work to be had and a nice life to make. Shook her to the roots when he was killed but priest never saw her cry. She'd come to church with beet red eyes and a quivering lip, but no tears were left for her public life. Now she worked at the church when she could, kept up with the day to day from her inheritance, helped with local children who needed it. Gave English lessons for money on the side, money she usually gave to the church.

'I like a woman of faith.' Sean'd polished off the wine.

Smiling and nodding now. Priest shoots him a crooked glance and he straightens up, takes the decency to blush. 'Terrible story, though. Poor woman's been through hell. Sounds solid though. Quite a woman.'

Priest shrugs and says something to himself. Sean jumps up with a start, sways a bit. 'Hell. Must be late. Better go check on Emma before it gets any later.' Tries to explain himself as best he can to the priest, who seems to get it, replies that he'll be asleep by the time he gets back. Blanket on the floor's his, buckets in the other room for washing. Sean nods and staggers out, feeling oddly guilty to feel so elevated in God's house. Well, He was the One turned water into wine, he thinks and smirks for his own cleverness.

On the way out, dodging pews and saints alike, he marvels at this woman, Bibiana. Couldn't say if he'd make it the way she has if he'd lost a wife. Might be that's why he never took one. Couldn't stand the thought of being attached to another person like that, of losing family again. Maybe. Kind of likes being attached to Emma, though.

Through the door and out into the dusty street and across, around the corner and there was her cottage. Thud of footsteps stops him. Looks round but doesn't see anything in the waning moonlight. Stops for a full minute but there's nothing. So he keeps moving and sees a shadow cross the drawn curtains of her window.

'Lord,' he whispers aloud and goes for his guns but his aren't there. Left them back at the church. Could it be Bibiana? Emma? Surely they were asleep by now and besides, no light came from the house. Long, purposeful strides took him around to her front door. Only thing there's his shadow, dim from moonlight, laying on the door. Does he knock? Barge right in? Second cup of wine wasn't necessary and now he's cursing himself for a fool. Listens for more steps but there are none, so he grits his teeth and grimaces, turns the knob and barges in.

Before he can take in the room, know what in the hell he's doing, a force gets him in the gut and and he's on his back and being pummeled by strong hands. All he can do to get his hands up and collect his wits long enough to sit up, grab his assailant and roll over. Raises his fist to break a nose, crack a face, anything, and it's her. Bibiana looks up at him, panting and wide-eyed, almost as wide-eyed as he is. There's a moment of blank confusion, neither knowing what to do and then, to his shock, she laughs. She laughs so hard that she has to gasp for breath. Laughing for relief, for the stupidity of the situation and her own foolishness, for this handsome, foreign man ready to give her a black eye. So Sean laughs too. Rolls off her first and collapses to the ground laughing.

'You always keep your doors unlocked?' he manages between laughs.

'I thought you were...intruder. I was going...for my gun...to...kill you!' And now the laughing explodes anew and Emma's there in the doorway, looking across the tiny kitchen to the tiny sitting room where there are two grownups lying next to each other laughing in the dead of night. It's a confusing thing, but she thinks it's alright so she walks over slowly, groggily and sits on the floor.

'Hey!' Sean bursts and reaches out, rubbing her arm.

Bibiana smiles. 'She has been sleeping. Sorry to wake you, pobrecita.'

Girl's smiling weakly, sheepishly. She wants to laugh, too, but doesn't know how. Doesn't know what they were laughing at and can't join in. So she just sits and takes it in and wonders if this is what normal people do.

'Well,' Sean says. 'I've made a big enough ass of myself. Just wanted to check and make sure everything was okay before I went to bed.'

The woman nods, still smiling. 'Smells like Father Orellana let you into his wine.'

'Just the sacrament, madame.'

'Of course.'

She finally gets a good look at him, even in the dim light. Short brown hair, going gray. Shabby beard that she hopes he trims whenever he bathes. Eyes, green and deep set and thoughtful with lines in the corners. Lines when he smiles, too. She likes that. She likes him. No. She pushes it away. She just likes the thought of a foreigner barging into her life with a little girl joined at his hip. Just likes the idea of a man, a good man, coming and shaking up her little world. She's liked that idea for a long time, long enough to wish it could come true quickly.

No, she doesn't like this one.

9. NEW LIFE

Next day he wakes up wincing, wishing he hadn't taken that second cup of wine. Not a serious hangover, just a headache he could do without. Headaches like that come easy when you drink about half the water you ought to each day. Water's not easy to come by in the desert or on a ship. Takes a moment to wonder how many lost sailors caved and drank water from the Sea, they were so thirsty. Luckily he's got a basin, and Priest is nowhere in sight so it's all his.

Sunlight lumbers in nicely as he rises. The small quarters are dimly pleasant, just as they were last night by candlelight, just as they were when he'd stumbled in after his encounter with Emma and Bibiana. The parting had been awkward. He wanted a kiss, knew he couldn't have one, but his wine-struck mind thought the possibility was there somewhere. The result was a man lingering too long for his own good, never making a move either to kiss or to leave. Just a lot of 'Well's and 'Okay then's after Emma'd gone back to bed and the small talk had died down and finally she had to say, 'I must get to sleep, Mr. Denman. Good night.' A stumble through the dark church, with a toe stubbed three times over, muttered curses, and then a collapse onto his blanket. Feels sure that he'd hoped he hadn't woken Priest before he fell asleep.

Since the tiny room's all his, he does the washing up he

hadn't yesterday. Scrubs his face, dunks his hair, dares to use the straight razor Father Orellana had left. Just takes the edge off his new beard, though, can't risk cutting himself too bad. Strips down, scrubs himself without making too big a mess, notes a new scratch on his arm and an old scar on his hip. Can't even remember where they came from, doesn't think it matters, wonders if it should. Turns away from the mirror and the basin and thankfully puts on a set of loaned clothes. Just brown trousers and a white shirt, but it's a godsend after so much time in his filthy digs. He wonders where to put his dirty clothes, or where he can have them washed, when Priest walks in.

'¡Buenos días, Sean!'

'Buenos días, padre. ¿Donde poner estos?' Holds up the clothes and Priest holds out his hands, offering to take them. He hopes the priest doesn't mean to wash them himself as he hands them over. Better to accept the hospitality either way. Explains that he's going to see Emma, then his horse, then he remembers he's famished. Priest motions for him to follow and leads him to the wholesome smell of bread, which leads him to the bread itself, steaming and fresh. Bibiana'd brought it over earlier but it's still warm.

'Woman even makes fresh bread in the morning,' he mutters.

Priest leaves him to break his fast and he does, quickly and noisily. He wants to get this day on. There is too much to think through, too much to figure, and if he can get some kind of jump on it then he just might have a whiff of direction before the night comes. Downs some water, wipes his mouth, and he's off, plodding through the now sunlit church with strong purpose, all fears left on his blanket with the night.

Ω

Emma opens the door of the small cottage for him. Looks happy for a girl who's not smiling.

'Pretty dress,' he says. Poor girl absently runs her hands down the thing, looks down at it self-consciously. Fits right. Light blue with a flowery pattern on it. Awful fashionable for the times, especially in a place like this. He'd meant it as a joke, having her pegged for a tomboy, but she does look lovely in a dress. Maybe the tough façade's on its way down with immediate danger left at Sea. No. She's tough alright, he thinks. She could wear a tutu and still be tough as nails.

'Good morning,' she finally says.

Sean's taken aback. Tips his silly bowler cap before he notices it and puts it back on, now conscious of the silliness. 'Morning to you, ma'am.'

And like that Bibiana appears behind her, smiling at her work. They're in decent places, in polite society. A local man simply calling on a local woman and, perhaps, her child. An earnest attempt at making nice, all thoughts of strangers and murder and alien necklaces far away.

'English teacher indeed!'

Bibiana looks surprised, motions for him to come in.

'Padre told me a little bit about you last night. Tongue loosens up after a little of that sacramental wine.'

She doesn't miss a beat. 'It was not sacramental wine. Why were you asking about me?'

'Well,' he laughs a bit. 'Got to know who's minding my girl, here. Though maybe I ought to have just waited. First sight of her clean and dolled up's all the evidence I need... not that there was ever any doubt.'

She smiles like a wolf. 'If you were asking about me then you ought to know my English is good enough for me to know tone. Flirty is like a tone of speaking, yes?'

'Yes, I suppose so.'

'Yes. I even know a few idioms! Like, "reach exceeding grasp." That's one, right?'

He laughs again to buy himself some time, though he is genuinely impressed. And mortified. Got to make sure she's not playing with him, and that he can remember what 'idiom' means. She is playing with him. Emma sits at the table, amused though she's only getting about a third of the conversation. She likes seeing Sean squirm a bit.

'Thank you for the breakfast. Bread was very tasty... and very needed.'

'You're welcome,' and she makes a little superfluous curtsy. They sit down now, pleasantries being out of the way. She even offers him coffee, which he takes all too readily.

'Your home is even lovelier in the daylight.'

'Yes, I'm glad nothing was smashed in our encounter last night.'

'Me too. Sorry, again.' Slips out of his flirty tone. Wasn't serving him too well anyway. 'You can imagine how edgy I've been, looking after her and what's happened and all.'

'That, and the wine.'

'And the wine.'

They smile at one another for a moment. Her cutting wit now more charming than disarming. The smile lingers in silent warmth until Emma slurps her coffee loudly.

'Children get coffee in this country?'

Bibiana nods, bemused.

'All the better. We'll be going to see Good Heart shortly. The horse, mean to say.'

Emma beams and manages to squeeze out 'Good!' through her thick accent.

Sean's got to smile at that. This girl's definitely got

more English than she let on. People in this part of the world got to speak more than one language anyways, what with occupiers and traders and neighbors moving around so close together. Maybe not here, though. Beyond the town and the big cities it's peaceful, like where he was before. That's his aim. It finally pokes through his clouded thought, though he knew it'd been there the whole time. Find some place quiet out here. Got to be enough money, even if it's the wrong kind of coin. Find some place. A ranch, raise horses, plant some fields or the like. Settle down. Strangers'd have to search the countryside over to find them. And if they did, if they were that persistent, well then he'd have a home to defend.

'...and my lessons should be starting shortly,' she's saying.

'Lessons?'

A pause. 'Yes, English lessons. Remember? Or did the wine take that one away, too?'

'Well, no. Certainly not. But you're coming with us. You'd like it better than teaching English. Terrible language, that, and Good Heart's one hell of a horse.' Her raised eyebrows say he ought to check himself for the coarse language and the swagger. 'What I'm trying to say is, we'd be awful fond of your company. Would you please care to join us?'

'That's better. I will see if I can...reschedule my morning lesson. The traders, whose children I teach, understand negotion.'

He thinks of correcting her. Negotiation. Thinks better of it and tips his ridiculous hat instead. Got to be enough money in his purse for a new hat. 'You ready, girl?'

Emma raises her eyebrows and nods, stands with him, and out they go, Bibiana watching. Emma takes his hand as they cross the threshold.

Ω

The stablemaster swears that horse would talk if given the chance, or so Sean interpreted.

'She's a good beast,' he says, having given up on Spanish for the moment.

Good Heart's prancing about the paddock, likely dreaming of open plains and sweet grass instead of the dry, dusty hay she's been eating. They lean, the three of them, propped against the fence of the stableyard, admiring the beast and the noon sun and the hills far beyond. Even the town at their backs, so very near, adds something to the scene. Sean'd had to refuse yet more coffee from Sideburns, for himself and on Emma's behalf. The girl'd almost gone for the proffered cup, but Sean was not ready to deal with a young girl hopped up on three cups of strong Spanish coffee. Good Heart seemed to be well taken care of; Sideburns the stablemaster took the liberty of redoing her shoes, brushing her out, and even checking her teeth. There's only one other horse at the stables, an old stallion called Copa who liked the shade of his stall more than the open air, so Good Heart got all the attention. The old horse was probably just weary of the small paddock and too tired for long rides in the hills.

Not Good Heart, though. She's born to run and Emma wants to be part of that, to feel what she felt across the Sea. So even in her skirt, having no idea what side saddle is, she grabs the works and walks out into the yard. Sideburns stands up, like he's going to stop her, until Sean lays a hand on his shoulder. Doesn't take his eyes off the girl, just watches, hopes the saddle's not too heavy, hopes against hope that she's got what he thinks she's got. Good Heart trots right up to her, stops with the girl at her flanks and shakes her head with a snort. It's just then, as she's putting it on the horse, that Sean gets a decent look at the saddle. It's all black. Gold lettering scratched along its rim. It felt so much like any other saddle that he'd not given it a second glance but something about seeing it in the daylight, really having a look with no distractions, gives him an odd feeling. Looks fairly normal: pommel and horn, fender, cantle, back housing. But there's no padding under the skirt. Makes a note to check it later and admires the girl throwing it onto the horse, checking the strap, making sure it's tight but not too tight while the horse endures it patiently, even kindly.

Meanwhile, Emma's nervous as a gnat. Just what was I thinking? she asks herself. I don't know how to do this. Probably end up hurting this horse. She looks up, face determined and sweaty, locks eyes with Good Heart. No. She smiles. This one is too tough for that.

She lightens, physically. Checks the strap one more time and prays she's done it properly. Checks the stirrups and wishes she had some kind of box to stand on. Before she can attempt to swing into the saddle Good Heart's on the move, walking over to the sturdy fence and sidling up to the beams in courtly fashion. She almost laughs. Backs up to the fence and raises herself up, gets one foot in the saddle and swings the other over. Almost overshoots, slips sideways and feels her heart jump. Sees Sean start from across the paddock. Steadies herself and waves and Good Heart is off at a slow trot and she calls out, whooping for joy and fear. Sean laughs and smacks the fence like it's a poker table and he's just won his life's savings back. Even Sideburns cracks a grin.

The girl could have ridden all day, felt the wind in her face and the bounce of the saddle, even when the soreness sets in she doesn't care. Doesn't care that they're riding in circles, barely at a canter. The joy of it's on her, and it's not the kind of thing you toss down. Much as he wants to watch her ride all day and let that feeling sink into her bones, they've got things to do and decisions to make.

Masked strangers come to mind.

And somebody in his head is saying things, things like, 'It's over. It was just the one. It's far away, under miles of water. You're safe and you've got a beautiful woman back there who just might be fool enough to have you.' Then Sean feels his heart catch again, the all-to-familiar anxiety sweeping over him like so much desert wind. Squinting, he sees the inlay work on the saddle is the same design as the pendant. Those other somebodies in his head wag their chins and cross their arms and declare it's time to pick up stakes. Even one day is too long, too long until they've got it settled.

But he can't let her stop just yet. Sideburns has set out some low bales of hay, even a low bar, and the girl's just about beside herself happy. Good Heart hops over them with ease, as if she's only jumping a bit for the goodness of the day. Sean whistles and the stablemaster comes over. Asks him where he can get some supplies. New clothes, maybe even a suitcase or satchel. So happens there's a tailor back in town, reasonably priced. Turns out Sideburns' real name is Castillo and he says that this place in town is the best. 'El mejor!' he proclaims. Sean doesn't much care. He needs new town clothes and new riding clothes and, for God's sake, a new hat.

They're walking back to the busier part of town, now. Buildings get closer together and cast magnificent shadows to keep the wretched heat off just a bit. Brown brick, white adobe, red tile roofs. Little balconies peer out into the streets and more than one citizen emerges to catch some cool air. Emma's still mad at him. Took minutes of protesting and arguing before he'd got her off the horse and minutes more to get her to follow.

'Bibiana. I Bibiana,' she'd said.

'No, by God, you're with me. We'll see Bibiana later.'

Doesn't understand, he thinks. If she's alone and without me and something happens it's my fault. Hard enough leaving her elsewhere last night.

Her arms are crossed and her eyes scowl but she's with him. Or at least a few steps behind him. He'd promised her a new dress or pants or whatever-the-hell she'd like, but it doesn't make much of a difference. Town's quiet, least this part is. No ships today so it's just the denizens making their way among white houses that peep out at the Sea. They come upon it fast. A house, white just like the others, with a red bird painted on it. *Sastre. Tienda de ropa.* Waits for Emma to catch up then slings his arm in hers and smiles through his annoyance and her obstinance.

'Clothes.'

Nothing.

'You can keep this stupid hat, if you like.' And he dumps it on her head, hard so it covers her eyes. A smile forms under the brim.

They pass the threshold of the shop and look for a while. The tailor isn't too keen on what he sees so he doesn't offer to help. They pass through the pants and shirts and boots and stumble into a slight piece of heaven: more hats than Sean's ever seen. There is a dubious variety, styles from all over the western world. Open crowns and flat brims, kettle curl brims, sagebrush crowns. Town hats, cavalry hats, cordobés and other sombreros. White, tan, brown, chocolate, black, and all shades in between.

Smiles in awe and mutters, 'I owe Castillo a coffee,' and starts looking.

She's looking, too. Fancies herself a rider now and if she's going to be one she's got to look the part. The sombreros cordobés catch her eye immediately. She likes the black, likes the flat crown and brim and the ribbon. Thinks it looks feminine without belonging to a Pasha's daughter. She holds it, moves it around in her hand, puts it on and immediately the shopkeeper materializes with a frown like a walrus.

Sean makes nice. Got to cover his tracks with some common courtesy since he looks like an ass in his borrowed shirt, which is too big, and slacks, which are too tight. And the silly bowler's hat. Shopkeep picks up on his accent, or lack thereof.

'You want new hat?' he asks.

'Well, yes.'

Shopkeep eyes him up and down, sizing him up as if for a fight.

'New shirt? Trousers?'

'Yes and yes. Decided on a hat already.' Hands him a Dakota hat that fits just right, black with a bound kettle curl brim. Emma steps forward and confidently hands him the sombrero.

'Two hats, then,' says Sean.

Emma holds up two fingers, just to show she understands. Shopkeep don't do much but raise his eyebrows. Then Sean produces some coin.

Minutes later he's in their pockets. Sean's been measured and the tailor's got shirt after shirt, new jackets and used, all laid out on the rack. He shakes his head or nods with great discernment, remembering now just how much cash he's got to spend on a few new pieces. Shirts are the easy part: solid white. One khaki, the other light cotton. Picks a black town suit with a waistcoat and a pair of brown riding pants. Throws in a new kerchief for good measure. Tells the man he's got to think about new boots. He clinks a few coins on the table, tells him he'll decide later about the boots and that the clothes go to the church once they're altered.

'You...giving these clothes?'

'Nope. Just staying at the church for the day.'

Shopkeep nods but doesn't understand. Doesn't really care. This is the first proper customer, and one with any taste, he's had in days. He hands Emma her hat with a smile.

'Ladies' shop is one street away. Me cousin, he make it. Tell him Set tell you.'

They walk out with their new hats and the odd satisfaction of purchase. Rather a step up from ragged passengers on a shady fishing vessel wearing clothes five days sour. And Sean's still got money to burn. Has to remind himself that he means to set up shop somewhere out in the country, got to have the money to buy or build a ranch, get some stock and all that stock needs. The road ahead's long and fraught with room for misstep. Uncertainty pokes at him and they stop in the middle of the street and he tosses and catches a handful of coins, the symbol of decision.

'Wait here. Or, wait outside the shop.'

She protests in her language.

'Can't afford all those clothes I just bought.'

And like that he's back inside and explaining himself and the tailor looks like he's going to burst.

'Well it's not like I took away any of your customers!'

'You have my time! I make clothes! I fit clothes! But not when I am with you!'

[89]

'I'm real sorry. I just got swept up. All this hat's fault. Which I am keeping!'

Tailor counters with the grimmest, deadliest stare Sean'd seen east of the Sea.

'And the riding clothes...but that's it!'

He opts to buy off the awkward silence. Slaps a few coins on the countertop, about a third of what he would have spent once the fancy town clothes were delivered. If it takes the edge off, the shopkeep don't show it. Just stares with a brewing resentment behind his eyes. Kind of man you'd hate to be across the card table from. So he hedges his bets and backs out slowly. Doesn't plan to go see his cousin at the ladies' shop.

Ω

'I...well, we've got a lot of things ahead of us, y'see. And we need all the money and if I got to wear the same old clothes for a while then that's just that.' He's waving his arms in exasperation, like swirling the air will summon some spirit to help him explain things to Emma. She gets it, just can't accept it.

'You are...look...dirty,' she says with genuine concern.

'Except for the hat.' Tips it at her, earns himself a smirk. 'Plus those new riding clothes'll be ready—'

'Bibiana!'

Looks up, squinting against the noon sun, sees the last of the streets leaving town. Church's just a block ahead, ranch is beyond city limits off northwards, to his right, and that heavenly woman is approaching them in a black town dress. Solid black, skirts high enough to not get trampled, long sleeved to keep the sun off. Got to smile. But she's not smiling and he's got about half a block to get it together.

'Like her, don't you?'

Emma smiles and nods, fixes her hair under the new hat.

'You want to stay with her, don't you?'

Smile goes away. Doesn't look at him or nod or shake her head, just keeps those green eyes focused on the forthcoming figure, the one woman in her life. Thinks about what she could teach her, thinks about life without a mother. Sean's thinking of a phrase about something like a 'woman's scorn' because now that they're close enough he can see an unhappy look on that comely face. He tips his hat again quickly, smiles like a diplomat.

'Well! I'm clearly unversed in the ways of the horseman. If I cancel my morning lesson to meet him on the ranch, it must mean something else for he's gone when I arrive!'

Sean blanches, tries to cover his tracks, 'Fair words. You ought to teach me English.'

It doesn't work.

'I'm sorry,' he says. 'All the things I want done hit me at once, you see, and...I just...it just slipped. I'm sorry.' Gets a scowl for his trouble, but that scowl's like the wind off an angel's wings coming from her. Fights a smile. 'Allow me to make it up to you. Let's have lunch together at the ranch. On me. Get to let Emma show off her new hat on Good Heart, too. We'll make sandwiches.'

She makes him wait, but just for a second or two. 'Alright, Mister Denman. You are lucky that I am a forgiving woman. But we will not have sandwiches. If you are going to be then you are going to eat like you are here.' Holds out her hand. 'Come, Emma. We will make lunch then meet your f— ...meet Sean at the ranch. Lunch will be on me.'

He looks down for the awkward embarrassment, notes Bibiana blushing a bit. Could be worse. Far worse a man could be called than the father of a lovely girl. Still glad her English isn't up to snuff.

Emma takes Bibiana's hand without a thought. Feels the strangeness of the moment but she's not sure why it's there. Takes a good look at Sean who's looking at Bibiana. Tips his new hat proudly and they're on their way.

♘

'Leaving tomorrow morning, padre.'

The blank stare reply causes him to rephrase.

'Mañana yo y la chica, vamos a ver. Salir.'

Priest nods with a bit of solemnity. 'Lo sabía,' he says. *I know.* Wishes him God's grace and blessing and tells him he's got a place to stay any time he needs it. Also reminds him that his clothes will be clean tonight. There's more, but Priest wants to wait. Thinks he ought to write it down. That way the American will have time to piece it together, and not miss anything. For the interim he pats Sean on the shoulder, walks with him out the door.

'Quieres almuerzo?'

Priest shakes his head. No lunch for him; man's got priestly things that need doing. Priestly things like shining the pews, cleaning out the latrine, tidying the confessional's cobwebs. Sanctifying the holy place for the unholy to come and take refuge in.

Sean tips his hat again. Tips it to everybody between church and ranch. Total of six people. Six people who get to notice his proper, new hat. One smile out of six ain't bad. And then he's there, the small, adobe ranch with the small barn in the shade of the Portuguese oak. Bibiana and Emma are already there, laying out a blanket with Castillo smoking idly on the porch, like a little pocket painting of home. Precisely what he wants. Just the afternoon of his second day here and the feeling's more homely than most feelings he's felt since he was a kid. Can't say if that's a good sign or just a sign or just a feeling. Either way, he don't mean to let it pass by.

'What have we got here?'

Bibiana smiles up at him like a vision in a dark blue dress. 'Potatoes, soup.'

'Looks perfect.'

She opens up the clay containers, finds some wide, shallow bowls and starts spooning food on them. Spiced potatoes with onions. Spoons the soup over top. Can't imagine how they got the things over here without spilling it all on the way here but there's no soup trail to be followed. Lunch is something out of a big city magazine. They lounge easily. Castillo brings out a pitcher of water with glasses and joins them. Even has lemons for the water. Bibiana chats him up like a courtier. Seems it's been some time since he was in the presence of a proper lady. Enjoys the niceties and the pleasant, easy conversation about the weather and the goings-on of the town. Sean tries to keep up but it's like trying to remember a dance step underwater, especially at the rate they're tearing through words. And yet their soup gets finished while he's sitting there, mid-bite, deciding which tense they're using, and there's Emma, not minding one bit, eating the spicy, garlicky soup eagerly. Decides she's easier noontime conversation.

'Tomorrow morning we're gone.' Tosses his thumb backwards to make his point.

Girl finishes her bite and waits. Waits like it's a matter of the soup reaching her belly before she can speak. But instead of speaking she just nods. 'Bibiana.'

'What about her?'

'She go.'

'No. I don't think so. I mean, I'd like it. Wouldn't you like it?'

Nods as eagerly as she eats.

'But to pack up and come with the likes of us, knowing us just one day. Doesn't work like that. Still...' Looks over at her and catches her eye. She smiles at him, Castillo laughs for some joke and he knows he wants her. 'No, that takes time.'

'You here. For her. Despues.'

Sean nods. 'Yeah. I think so. And...I know you want to stay with her. But I also think you know that I can't let that happen. If they come back. The men. The strangers. That's on me.'

Doesn't say anything. Just slurps down the rest of her soup.

'Mister Denman, Mister Castillo was just saying that he thinks your horse must be the best in this part of the country. Where did you find him?'

Sean takes his time biting off a hunk of flatbread, makes sure it's well chewed while he measures his answer. 'She was a gift. And, no, I never looked her in the mouth.'

Not so much as a titter. He'll have to teach them that expression.

'Just a gift?'

'Kind of sad, must say. A dying man wanted to pass her on to someone good. And when she took a shine to Emma and me, we all knew it was likely meant to be.'

'That's a good story.' She breaks away to explain for Castillo, who turns his gaze to Sean and smirks like he knows something Sean doesn't. Sean doesn't like it, shrugs it off as paranoia, thinks it's time to end this idyllic lunch and go for a ride. Been almost three days since he's ridden Good Heart and that one sprint to the Sea was enough to rekindle a fire long smouldering.

'Speaking of the beast,' he says and wanders off to the barn. Emma's face lights up. Stuffs another hunk of bread in it before chasing after Sean at a sprint. Widow and rancher chat as neighbors do, but the latest neighborly gossip is cut short by a whooping call and the clatter of barn doors. Good Heart bolts out, a spotted flash against the bright day. Rider's practically unnoticed. Leaps the fence, dashes clear across the yard to the other side, and leaps that too.

The onlookers stand up. Maybe there's a problem. Horse and rider bolt off beyond the few oaks, gnarled and wise, off towards nowhere. Copa, the old stallion, pops his head out of the barn window. Then there's the girl standing on the fencepost, calling out, smiling, waving her hat. No problems here. Just a rider needing to ride and a horse as needs the free air. They go. When the watchers think the going's gone the gallop breaks left, shadows shift and move back towards the ramp. Sean's tucked in tight, head down for catching the wind against the brim, pushing the hat down firm against his dome. Won't be no losing this one. Slows to a canter, then a trot, then stops dead on the far side of the fenced yard. Horse hops lightly, huffing. Rider slips down, hands the reins to the fast approaching girl. Copa neighs from the window, sounding more alive than he has in a long time. Sean meets Bibiana around the paddock.

'That's all?'

He laughs at that. 'Just a spurt, ma'am. Had to get it out. Think the horse did, too.'

She nods. Truthfully, she's impressed. Always been taken with riders but only dabbled herself. She sees, maybe, this man as he's meant to be seen. But she keeps it on the inside.

Ω

Afternoon's drab and lazy, but the right kind. After lunch they sipped coffee, compliments of Castillo the rancher, who didn't believe in afternoon naps. Emma's a believer, though, and slept for the better part of the afternoon in the grand shade of the Portuguese oak. Plates on a blue coverlet, porcelain cups rest on the uncomfortable ground. Sean finds it hard to take his ease. Things are on his mind. Not the dark things of recent days, but the future that's been lingering there for a while, before Jack, before Emma. Castillo gets up to see to the horses. Or to leave them alone. Either way, things are silent save for the soft and steady breathing of the girl. Leaves blow off the trees and fall drowsily down. The woman minds herself, smiles contentedly, but silence grows beyond its intention. Sean feels it, fights it back, decides it's time to say the things as need saying.

'Will you walk with me?'

'Emma might be startled to wake alone,' she says.

'We'll keep in hailing distance. She's out, leastways.'

Helps her up. Makes bold and holds her hand for a bit. She feels his tension, but feels relaxed herself, so she doesn't quite understand. Their footsteps make no noise and he lets go of her hand.

'I don't rightly know how to say what I'd like to. This is as strange a time as any man can imagine having. But I mean to leave at first light tomorrow. With Emma.'

Her eyes say she was expecting that. 'I did not think you'd spend much time roofed under a church.'

'No. Padre's a fine man and helpful, but…I feel the need to move. I can't say all, but I have friends further west, beyond the bluffs. Reckon they can help me set up shop.'

'What kind of shop?'

'I mean to find some land. Get a few horses. Maybe lease out some fields to planters. This land's just right for it.'

'So you will not go home.'

'See no need for it.'

Her expression gets stern. Brows contort. 'I don't understand it in full, but I know that you are pursued. Come, it is obvious enough I think, that you didn't leave your troubles behind in the desert. And Emma had horrible dreams last night. She awoke several times but before that she called out in her language. The only word I could understand was "stranger". Please don't insult me by denying it. You told me you thought there were men after you, men that killed her father. If there is such a...haste upon you then why not go all the way? Go back across the Sea to America?'

'With a girl in my charge? Can't say that suits me. Besides I've more a place here than back home, I believe. We'll be alright. But I can't say I know much in the way of rearing a child, much less a girl on the brink of womanhood. It would...mean to say, I would appreciate...it would be good if we could call on you, time to time.' Takes her hand in his. 'Best if *I* could call on you.'

Her face speaks pain, confusion, happiness all at once. Kind of look one gives when a child is born, but born sick. All that calm leaves her. She suddenly wants to hold his hand again. Sees a future, but a risky one. Her desires are no longer those of a silly girl, but of a whole person willing to risk all for the chance of wholeness.In the end it's her heart that betrays her, one that has been broken too many times. That old desire is tamped down once more and her fingers flutter and she says, 'I will be here...for the girl.'

Ω

He awakes with the Sun next morning. The little cot in the little room he shares with the priest is already becoming too comfortable. Takes a proper bath this time, foregoing the wipe-down. But his heart's heavy. Feels like a hangover. Emma'd woken up just after his little talk with Bibiana. They'd parted ways quietly, the girl staying with the woman, the horse with the rancher. Man walks the short trip back to town in the calm evening breeze on his own. Once in town he'd walked for seeming hours. Just as soon as the Sea found him, twinkling gold in the setting sun, that eerie, cold feeling struck. It creeped between his shoulders and on down. But no evil men were in sight despite his itchy trigger finger. No strangers, light eyes under hats and above scarves, found him. He chalked it up to rejection and fatigue and the weariness of this week.

He kept on walking, down to the piers where the boats come in. Through the market where he bought something sweet. Round through the shops and slums and alleyways and on back to the eaves of the town where the warm church welcomed him back. No wine that night. Just quiet contemplation.

Priest must've been on about his duties, coming after sleep took him and leaving before it let him go. So he bathes alone, finds his own clothes clean and pressed. Meager possessions go in the meager bag and the gunbelt fits snug around his hips. Still, it looks odd; one old flintlock and an enameled revolver. He figured that's what it must be, fingering the barrel and the breeches and the grip in his bed the night before. Enamel to make it look the way it does, so alien and beautiful. On his way out the door he notices the Lord hanging over the frame. To Him he prays he won't have to use those guns again. And that that woman might have a change of heart.

Ω

Emma opens the door to the cottage in a black riding dress. Hair's pulled back tidily and her face is broad and clean. He gives her a hug out of instinct, which she welcomes.

'This is what we call "early rising",' he says and she nods with a forced smile.

Girl doesn't really want to go. Don't really want to stay either but she knows she's got to stick with him and with Good Heart. The two of them won her her freedom and her life and she knows Bibiana isn't gone for good. Can't shake it, though, the sound of the woman sobbing in the night at the edge of the bed. Woke her up and at once her heart took off and she tensed, ready to flee pale men or crude sailors. Just sobs, though. Tears for womanly things she cannot understand or hope to just yet. Thought of comforting her, holding the older woman. Thought better of it. We're all of us entitled to private sorrows and, like that, the woman's there, in the flesh. Radiant and tall and broad-shouldered and brown in blue. She isn't smiling but Sean is. Beams at her like a fool. Hopes the grin props up his heart like he wants it to.

'Coming to see us off at the ranch?'

'No,' she says. 'You will have my prayers and best wishes from here.'

Tips his cap. 'You've got my thanks for the kindness you've shown us. You're a remarkable woman.' Emma watches the exchange. Watches Sean take her hand and grip it fiercely and say, 'Understand, Bibiana...I'm no quitter' and watches tears arrive in her hard, set eyes.

They get wiped away and she says 'I won't encourage you to.'

The moment flies away quick as it came.

'Let's go, girl,' he says and they're off with Bibiana in the doorway. Wants to say goodbye to Priest but he's nowheres to be found. Must be some kind of priestly emergency, he thinks. Maybe the Pope's in town. And then there's a 'Wait!' called from the little cottage and Bibiana's in the doorway and then she's through the doorway, running them down with a book in her hand.

'Something to pass the time,' she says and hands it to him and it says *The Spanish Language*. Smiles and nods his thanks. Emma looks at her with wishes. When Sean turns and goes and puts some distance between them she waves and trots to catch up.

Ranch's even quieter than the rest of the city. Castillo's paid up. No need to wake him, so they head on over to the barn and see Good Heart's head poking out of the window like a kid looking for Santa Claus. Long white beard's gone brown and the red shirt's a dusty black but it's all the same to the horse, the best present of all: time to ride.

'Got you a present,' he says. 'A gift.'

Emma cocks an eye at him, either suspicious or not understanding. Inside the barn he walks past Good Heart's stall and opens the last one and walks out with Copa, the old stallion, by the reins. He's suited up in saddle and tack, even got new shoes. Shakes his head anxiously.

'For you!' Sean declares and Emma laughs her sweet joy.

Evening's come and there are no more tears for Bibiana. She's cried enough in her life. Now she's waiting, either for the world to come around to her or for God to present a sign. Got to be a sign somewhere on this road, on her porch, sipping tea as the sun sets at the end of that long day. Sipping calm like, deliberate, every motion of her arm, cup to saucer, cup to mouth, cup to saucer, perfect with its direction and trajectory. This is when things are best, in the quiet of the evening, when the noise from the city is dying away and she can see the Sun seeking its rest. That Sun won't illumine any signs this day. God always gives us tomorrow, though, she thinks, and decides two cups of tea is enough if she expects to get to bed, expects to sleep amid the toss-and-turn in her mind. To be reckless, to fly and make a life with a man she barely knows, or to live as she always has.

And then there's a man. He's standing in the middle of the road, just beyond the corner of the adjoining house. Small from Bibiana's vantage point and odd looking. Notices him and almost starts. Can hardly see anything but a wide-brimmed hat and a scarf that covers everything but his eyes. Looks like a great black line over his eyes. Thought, even hoped, it was Sean for a moment by his height and posture. But that's not Sean. Just a stranger staring at her. She remembers her rifle and is about to go and get it when he waves and wanders off in the direction of the docks. She gets the gun anyway, prays until well past her customary bedtime, and sleeps fitfully.

10. ABEL

Hooves thump the soft, dry ground. Sounds like the clanging of a hammer on chains to Sean. Soon enough they're broken and he's free and he's kicking the sides of his horse riotously. No spurs, though. Never spurs and then he remembers that he's on Copa. The old stallion found a marked change in himself almost as soon as he left old Castillos sameness. Fast as he goes, though, fast as his new spirit will drive him, he's no Good Heart. Emma waves her hat at him from fifty yards ahead.

'Guess I'm her father now if I let her talk me into riding this slowpoke.'

The riding is smooth and easy, what he expected and what he was willing to let the girl try. Despite her enthusiasm, girl's still a novice at best and any harsher terrain would've unmade her. Even under Good Heat's care.

Away from the town, away from the Sea, the land opens up. Still brown and dusty and shrubby and beautiful, but wide and open. Trees and clumps of grass, once leaking out of the dirt like refugees, now stand proudly and closer together as if they'd found their place. They climb a rise and the town is a white speck behind them set against the black-blue of the Sea. She makes out a ship, a smaller white speck drawing near to the harbor, and shudders for some reason. Girl's not sure why, but everything feels right. Thinking on it too much she sees the illusion and knows she's on a chair teetering on top of a high building. The thrill of it crumples into fear. So she doesn't think, doesn't wonder. Just feels and on Good Heart she feels like a bird without care.

Father didn't think she could remember but she did. She was a tiny girl, who couldn't see onto the table, but she remembers, remembers the wax face of her mother on the wooden table top. It wasn't her mother, just her shell, her plastic doll, and the other women were cleaning her, praying to God and cleaning her. All she remembers is the face and the prayers, but she can't remember what she felt. Didn't really want to because what can a little girl feel that she should want to feel, now almost a woman? Then they covered her in cloth and she was gone.

She knew her mother had been buried, knew the men had carried her away and a few others had come and that they prayed and that they put her in the ground. But all she remembers is the wax face of her mother on the table being cleaned. She hates it, that that is the last memory of her mother. Now the wax face is practically blank. An anonymous mess with dark hair. Soon it would be gone and then Emma would be free.

Ω

In this moment, however, she is free. Sean is calling her now, telling her to wait, but she doesn't. She wants to be free and so she kicks Good Heart and whoops and Good Heart takes the cue and tears off into space, a mass of muscle and speed sure to burst into flame at any moment.

He's calling her again, louder, almost panicking. Now she knows why. The freedom exceeds control. Her heart pounds. Had she been a more skilled rider she'd have ducked low, peer out to steer Good Heart around the bumps and obstacles the horse wouldn't see, maybe keep her from jumping. Saddle's slipping away, or she's slipping away from it. World gets spinny, like there are breaks in her vision. She's looking at the sky, now Good Heart's mane, now behind her, now ahead. There's a fallen tree and she curses and that's all she remembers.

Sean sees it. Girl loses her footing as the horse jumps. Sees her slip out of the saddle and hit the ground but her foot is stuck so she bounces back up and hits the ground again and Good Heart stops and there's a cloud of dust and he's kicking Copa and cursing to the point of tears. Leaps off the old horse and rushes over, skids into the dirt and scoops her up, one hand on her head and the dirt clears. Sees she's smiling. She laughs. The crazy girl lets out a laugh and he wants to hold her close and kiss her and slap her and scream and laugh with her, all at once if he can. Her eyes flutter and he picks her up and leans her against Good Heart.

'Just what in the hell is the matter?' he shouts.

She giggles. Too relieved and frightened to bother with English.

'You're done. You won't be riding alone again for a damn long while.'

Hand on her forehead, she says something in her language. Rubs her eyes.

'Look at me.'

He checks her eyes and they seem okay. He's no doctor but he's seen men take a fall or get kicked. She doesn't have their eyes but she's got to have a bad bump at best. Feels around on top of her head, behind, and she winces. Right there, on top. Bet her neck hurts like hell, too. Best if they rest so they find a tree, sit in the shade and have some water while the horses graze.

Girl's still holding her head when he stands up to take a look round. Dead ahead, north and west, the patches of green spread out to overtake the land. Looks like they're at the top of a massive plateau and down at the bottom is green grass and trees and beyond those trees is Granja Esperanza and his friends and, he hopes, new life. Phrase actually seems to mean something right now, like it's not before. When he left home and came across the Sea, it wasn't for hope. Not 'new life' neither. It had been for fear's sake and loss and a quiet desperation. Now he's got something. And that something was dozing under the tree.

Dashes over, takes her head in his hands and says, 'Stay up, girl. No good falling asleep after a knock on the head like that.'

Struggles to get her eyes open, shakes her head, then squeals as a cup's worth of water lands on her head. Ought to wake her up, he thinks. And it does. She's on her feet and fairly livid. Livid's better than comatose.

'I think that's enough rest.'

Offers his hand and she takes it and they're both on Good Heart now with the girl up front. Easier to keep her awake. Takes Copa's reins and ties the sorrel to their saddle. Old horse seems glad to be done with the burden. They're off at a trot in the afternoon sun.

Sean wants to make it halfway before they camp but that's a high goal. Round the edge of the plateau they go, sheer at some parts, sagging at others. Feels sure there's some kind of incline they can make that way, to the right, though he's not sure why. Better than no direction at all. He's grateful for every patch of shade, feels his neck burning despite his fancy new hat. Grateful even more when he sees the ridge come to its sloping end.

They pick up the pace, Emma more alive now, taking

in all the landscape and ignoring the pain in her legs. Pain in her head's worse but there isn't time for pain when the world explodes in green and blue. Once down the incline, they come to an infinite valley, green with grass and shrubs and trees and yet somehow still brown. Crowns of bald hills poke up here and there, bursts of brown in the green and the dust. Good Heart bursts through the green herself, though she seems considerate enough to not leave Copa too far behind. Emma can imagine the grumpy old horse muttering to himself or yelling at Good Heart to slow down. Laughs to herself and Sean smiles. That's a good sign.

Riding's smooth for hours. Quiet except for the wind in the trees and the grass and the thud of horseshoes on the hard packed ground. Sooner than he'd believe, day is on her way out and they welcome the gloaming light of evening. Land's hardly changed at all. Like a sea of its own. Stars appear, the moon's beaming off a pond nearby. They dismount, Emma stumbling a bit. He checks the water. Tastes fine so they settle for the night, unroll blankets, even get a little fire going. Supper's crusty bread and some fruit, compliments of Castillo from the day before. They don't speak. Horses graze and stay close without staking. No more words, but they're both thinking it. Thinking of what happened last time they were camped out in the open. No more words, no more riding. If strangers are coming, they can come. They're too tired to care. They rest their weary legs and soon they sleep.

Ω

He should've known better, should've kept a closer eye on her. The sun's up, but she's not.

'Emma. Emma!' Calls her name but she doesn't wake. Breathing, but looking bad, looking gray in the face. He doesn't think twice about it because there's nothing to think about. He's not a doctor, he's a rider. He can ride to the doctor. Whistles and Good Heart's there in a moment, Copa following thoughtfully behind. Scoops her into the saddle and a second later he's behind her. Scoops up their bag, leaves the fire smouldering, says, 'Got to leave you behind, Copa. Follow if you can' and kicks Good Heart for all she's worth.

The miles are trod down like unwanted insects, unending lines of ants. Hills rise to the left and are gone before Sean can note the color. Trees fly by. The low mountains to their right aren't going anywhere, but they can stay; their course is dead ahead, straight as an arrow and Good Heart's the point. Copa kept up for a while, but began lagging behind. He'd either find them or find a new life in the wild. Or be a hefty dinner for a lynx. Sean didn't want to think about that.

She's still slumped in the saddle. He keeps a tight arm around her, the other holding the reins but only out of habit; this horse'd go wherever he asked with a whisper. Sun's high above them when the land starts looking familiar, like he might've been here before. Trees bending a certain way, bushes arranged just so. Another good sign, but the last good sign spoiled pretty quick so he waits out his luck. Land begins to rise again. There's a ridge dead ahead, leagues away, and he does count that a good sign. They don't pass a soul or, if they do, they're too fast to be seen. Good Heart's grunting from time to time but they don't stop. Plenty of time to rest once Emma is safe.

Then again, might not make it to safety if Good Heart drops dead. Even if she survived that, he might not survive the thrashing she'd give him if Good Heart was gone. So they stop. Good Heart drinks deep from a little pool. He just sits with her in his lap. Her head lolls and he frowns, but her mouth moves. A good sign?

Off again, even faster now. Maybe the horse senses the urgency. 'Let's go,' he says. 'Let's go! Come on!' and the ridge is closer, closer, closer and now he knows that beyond that ridge is what he's looking for. He curses, but his brain can't keep up with Good Heart; the fallen tree is cleared just as he recognizes it. He laughs for it, grips the girl tighter, prays that she'll be alright, that it's just her body recovering like a shut dandelion. But he can't fight the worry away, can't shoot it down because she looks pale. Her creamy brown skin now looks more like his, if not whiter. Fights on anyway, beating back the wild dogs of panic and fear. Even tries humming low tunes he knew from his childhood. Church songs. Stephen Foster. Even the unfamiliar ones he'd picked up in the desert.

It works. The ridge is upon them, grassy and gently sloping. Trees line the top, stretching out their long limbs for a taste of sunshine. The tobiano slows, huffs a bit of froth out, and takes the incline at an easy trot. Just like I'd have told her to, he thinks. Top of the ridge is much like the last, only broader. On the other side below the green is greener and wider, a true sea hinted with brown. Way down's much steeper than the way up but Good Heart knows the urgency and, apparently, the way down. Path's none too clear, but it's there and the horse makes easy work of it.

He can see the horizon now and the sun catching up to it. Just beyond the edge there, and to the south a bit, they're home free. Home free means the ranch where he once worked and there is Abel and Doña. Abel knew a thing or two about medical care, and he's hoping he's still got it in his brain, and that he's not started drinking today. Path winds here and there, always downwards. Tries to steer Good Heart when she seems to have lost it, but the horse gets stubborn, goes back up when she ought to go down. The trees, while no great wood, are thicker than before: bright oaks and spruces. Seem to throw her off somehow. Through the patchy wood the valley floor rests below, a little closer than before. But he can feel the tension in the horse so he pats her, says nice things and gently tugs the reins where he thinks she ought to go. Takes them close to thirty minutes to hit the bottom and he knows the horse ought to rest but he's too worried about his girl now. Spurs her on with his soft boots, prays she's as tough as she seems, that she can go leagues on a breath. Steers her to the left and it's a mad sprint to the finish.

The grass, brown and green now, flies by and the trees and now the rain fly by. Rain's almost horizontal but it's light and doesn't matter and the spatter hits Emma's face. Face contorts, just slightly, and like that, hope's in the saddle with them.

'Abel! Abel!'

Doña's the first to find them. Rushes out from around the corner where the well is, middle aged woman with the kindest face ever known.

'Sean!' she gasps. '¿Que paso?'

'Abel!' It's practically a scream now. 'I need Abel! ¿Donde es?'

She grabs the crook of his arm and leads him inside. The rest of his arm is carrying a girl she doesn't know, probably fourteen years old, and she's unconscious. Poor woman's scared for someone she's never seen before and a man whom she's not seen in weeks. Inside, throwing covers off the bed, pointing, going around back to the porch where she slaps the bottle of wine out of Abel's hands. He's young, younger than Sean, slender and handsome with a pencil moustache and goatee. He's not happy.

'¡Oye!'

She grabs him by the scarf around his neck and tells him to get it together, there's a sick girl inside. He asks for coffee. Inside he sees someone he never thought to see again.

'Thought that I ran you away, cowboy?'

But the man he sees is haggard, worn down, and hovering over a young lady. Holding her hand, looking down at her face with his own covered in fear. Abel takes a moment because he doesn't know what to do, what to say or think, and then it goes away and he kneels down beside the girl on the bed.

Calls for cold water. Hand pulls her eyelids open with one thumb. Sean watches him. Abel checks her eyes, touches her head in places, her arms and shoulders, takes her chin in his hand and tilts her head side to the side. Then her eyes move under her lids. Cold water arrives by one of stable hands and he wipes her dirty face, leaves the rag on her forehead. Looks up at Sean. Tries to remember how to say *bedside manner* in English.

'She will be okay, my friend,' he lies.

Sean immediately looks relieved. Puts his hand on Abels shoulder, squeezes and pushes off to stand. He's nodding quietly.

'I think she is contused in her brain, but I know not for sure. We must wait and see when she wakes up.' That's closer to the truth. The girl's in a coma and out here there isn't much to be done but wait.

So they wait. Couldn't have been worse timing for

getting back together with old friends, but he makes do. Won't leave the room, though. So Abel pours some of the water into some dusty glasses. Hard to keep the dust out with all the commotion. He hands it to him and he takes it and lifts it in the tiniest of toasts. Feels the water go down, washing away the dry dirt in his throat. Finally gets to looking round.

It's the same as he remembers; way too pretty for a ranch.

They'd come in through the brown door in the white wall of the kitchen, passed through the empty space to the low wall that divides the kitchen out from the sitting area, stepping over the immaculate brown speckled tile into the spot beneath the stairs where the daybeds were. Upstairs were the proper bedrooms for the owners and lifers. Stablehands slept elsewhere. But the remarkable thing about the house was its windows. They were arched, per the style of the day, but the glass was almost perfectly clear. Up on top, the arches were filled with a half-circle of stained glass. No particular images, just lovely patterns and such.

Sean collapses into a wooden rocking chair, presses the cool glass against his head and waits. Murmurs behind him. Spanish murmurs that he doesn't bother understanding because he's preoccupied: Abel's not a good liar. At least the last bit was true and he can't do anything now but wait and at least here the waiting will be comfortable. He was, he hoped, at the last stage. Journey's not over without the girl, though, and all the thoughts jump up about her being invalid or dead or dumb.

'I have one of the boys taking your horse.'

He nods. Doesn't even look at Abel sitting down next to him, wiping the sweat from his brow.

'I think you have quite the story to tell!'

'Not now.'

'Later. After dinner. We don't have a fatter calf for our prodigal son here, but we eat well later!'

'*Fattened* calf.' That was Abel in a nutshell. Missing *fattened* but saying *prodigal* perfectly.

'I've not had much English to try with you gone...you took my advice, didn't you?'

Nods again.

'You really aren't going to talk, are you?'

Doesn't get anything for his question, not a shake of his head or a disapproving look. Does get a glance at the guns on his hips, though, and wonders.

'Abel.' Doña calls for him, sets off some orders in rapid Spanish, as if they don't want to give Sean so much as a chance for interpretation. Gets up, pats Sean on the shoulder and vacates. Now it's just Sean, with Emma on the other side of the wide open house, alone with their dreams.

Ω

Outside is Doña with a stable boy. Ricardo's his name and he thinks Good Heart the best horse he's ever seen in all his sixteen years of life. Spent the last hour brushing the horse and feeding her peppermints. The woman's seeing to some laundry, airing out some bad thoughts along with the wash. She'd loved Sean dearly. Too young to be his mother, too old to be anything more, she'd privately curated an image as his loving aunt. Seeing him so distraught so suddenly was difficult.

She imagines him riding up for the first time with Nuñez, the trader from the nearest town and probably the only one there who spoke any English. Said he had an experienced rider (a real American!) looking for work and she'd taken him in. Thought he'd make a good foil to the wild Abel and he had. Evened out the unpredictable aristocrat well. Been like brothers and she their mother who couldn't be their mother. Hadn't been a mother at all. Unable to have children, she ran the ranch and its hands and helpers like a mother hen until her husband died and left the whole thing to her.

Doña is still mad at him for that.

She wanted to go to Madrid and from Madrid to anywhere else and now she is almost an old woman with nothing but horses and stable hands to call her family.

Tells Ricardo to go and make sure Abel is getting dinner sorted with the house girl, Yessenia, and the boy trots off, leaving her alone.

All around her is what rich people in the cities in America dream about: wide, green, hilly wonder sparkling in the setting sun. Nothing for miles. For her, the horizon is an invisible fence. The warm orange tones of sunset have gone cold.

But now, Sean is back. That must count for something. And who is this girl with him? Abel hadn't told her too much when he left. Sean had said something about a change, about the Sea, but she'd gone white like desert sand when he'd proclaimed his exit, didn't hear a whole lot of what he'd said. She was losing a son. She blamed Abel for his leaving, mostly, though she kept that inside, too. Just got cold towards him was all, waiting for her other son to return.

While the wind blew and whipped the trousers and shirts and towels here and there, she felt her heart kicking around as well, blown by the air of change. She didn't like it, but inside she liked it. In the end, this was all she had.

11. Home

Sean dreamed of the Sea, dreamed of Jack. Waves came and ate him up a piece at a time, each wave taking a bit more of Jack with it. Skin first, then bone. Waves with teeth like an animal. Waves turn from water to sand and Jack gets eaten up and when the last bite of his head happens gold comes out. Large gold coins and Sean can't tell if they came from Jack or the wave or the ground. When the coins hit the ground, they burst and out comes Emma flailing on the ground and screaming. Screams. Those screams are real. He can hear them and he wakes himself up and shoots out of the bed and is at the side of hers.

Girl's awake and upright and crying in her language. He shushes her, strokes her arm but she swats his hand away.

'Alright, Emma. You're safe here. It's alright.' Uses his best fatherly tone, but he's shaking. Whole house has got to be up now. She quiets down a bit, and finds a place in her hands for her face. Now Sean holds her, gets on the edge of the tiny bed. He can hear her murmuring, still in her language.

'You're okay, girl.'

'They coming,' she moans. Sobs are coming again, softer this time. She calms down. 'They here. *Jinn* coming.'

Chills attack his spine, up to his neck. 'No. No, Emma. We're safe here. They won't come.'

They hear footsteps and Sean screams inside,

commanding his heart and his nerves to calm down, roaring at them not to be afraid. It's just Doña or Abel coming to check on them. His heart sings a different tune, though. They are coming. Footsteps are on the stairs now and Emma shudders, closes her eyes, and digs her fingers into Sean and Abel appears looking as scared as they are.

'Santo de Dios,' he breathes. 'She awake?'

Sean nods and Abel walks over. Puts his candle on the table and squats at the foot of the bed. Works up a smile. Emma cracks an eyelid for him.

'This is Abel. He's a friend. He's a doctor...or, almost a doctor...anyways, he can help. Can he have a look at you?'

After a moment's silence Abel stands, approaches the side of the bed and Emma shakes her head. Clinging to Sean more tightly.

'Just...can this wait until morning?'

Abel looks reluctant. 'Yes. Just try and keep her awake. Sun is almost up.'

'We...eh, we were followed. I think we were followed. We ought to keep watch for anyone coming down the ridge.'

'Followed? Who?'

'Doesn't matter. Just get one of your kids to do it or something. This is serious.'

'I'll tell Doña. Then I'm going back to bed.'

And so, a few minutes after Abel left, Ricardo shows up downstairs, looking sleepy and hateful. Doesn't bother looking at them, just marches out the front door for his early guard duty. He'd be asleep in minutes. Sean gets up but she grabs his wrist and looks up at him pleadingly. Doesn't want him to go. She's been asleep so long, two days since they arrived at the ranch, and all she wants is some company. His company. Just for a while. He grants it.

Rubs a hand through his hair and against his eyes and sits back down and she smiles and pats him on the shoulder, then puts her head where her hand had been.

He's feeling annoyed and anxious and happy. Wants to be out there, looking. Doesn't want to wake up with evil men staring him down, guns drawn, but he does want to be here for his girl. Lets it go, feels it leave his body, the knowledge of coming death. She feels it, too. And then they're asleep.

℧

In the morning things look brighter. Takes some prodding, but Emma wakes up. Without screaming. Abel curses Sean, saying he took an awful risk letting her fall back to sleep. Ricardo says he saw nothing. Nothing but the back of your eyelids, Sean thinks. But he's pleased. Doña and the house girl work on breakfast. Smell of eggs and tomatoes and aught else. Ranching family gathers and Abel says, 'I think we need to hear your whole story from the beginning.'

Sean takes a long, thoughtful sip of coffee. Says, 'No. Not yet.'

'All right. Then why you were out here to start with?'

He just eats his eggs, bites off a hunk of bread in silence. Emma stares at the other girl through the kitchen door and wonders what her name is. Stable boys eat and rush out to the horses, eager to finish up. End of the working week's today and they'll go back to town to their families once the work is done.

'I'm looking for some land myself, Abel.'

Doña's ears perk up, even a room away.

'Land? You a farmer now?'

'No. I want my own place. My own horses. Might lease out the land for local farmers, if they want it.'

'That is very interesting!' A grin splits his pretty face.

'Why, I wonder?'

'Once in a while, a man's ready to settle down. Sometimes he's got to get out from under the wings of his mother hen.' Forces a smile as Doña enters.

She's not smiling. Just says something in Spanish to Abel.

'Isn't that why you left us before?'

'No. I was just...' Takes a minute. '...I was just restless. I think my feet kept wanting to move. I'd come so far, but something in me wanted to keep going.'

'You find anything out there?'

'Yeah...I found her.' He nods at Emma polishing off the last of her eggs. Likes being able to avoid conversations not in her language, even if she's getting the general idea. Doña pats her on the head.

'And who is she? The reason why you're settling down? Or is there somebody else?'

'By God, I think the only thing on your mind is girls.'

'Only thing on any man's mind is girls, amigo. Now I know I am right.'

Sean taps his finger on the table. 'Anyways. You know where I can get some land?'

'Sure. If you can pay.'

'I can pay.'

Abel slides back, makes a note in his mind to ask Doña about the land. 'So you found a girl, a woman, and some money out there. I may be going myself!'

'Found even more than that.'

'You also found a way to keep secrets. Not sure what I think of this new Sean.'

'Same as the old Sean.

'Tal vez,' he says. Perhaps.

Morning's spent perusing the ranch at a slow, comfortable pace. It's the same as it ever was before Sean left: just a few new boys and one girl from town helping things out. Like an informal apprenticeship. Kids get some food and learn how to handle horses, Doña gets some help. Ricardo's the obvious leader of the pack. Emma's with them, despite some protestations by Doña.

'¡Mujeres deben estar en la casa!' she said. Emma doesn't speak Spanish and Abel doesn't translate. The girl wants to see her horse. She hopes Yessenia will come with her, but the other girl won't avert her eyes from the washing up.

The stable is much like any other stable: low with a steepled hay loft on top. Twelve horse stalls. It almost didn't make sense, these few small buildings out at the top of a hill in a valley just outside nowhere, but even outside eyes would see that they fit just fine. Good Heart's up front. Abel opens the stall and Emma cuts in front of Sean, stands in the doorway, staring at the horse who stares back. And there's a moment for Sean. He's seen it before. Accidents happen and people can blame horses that aren't at fault. And for just a moment he's sure Emma will start yelling at Good Heart, mustering up every curse in her strange desert-tongue.

Doesn't happen, though. She hugs his neck. Doesn't even cry. She does say something he can't hear or understand. And like that, they're done, like two brothers forced to hug by their mother after a fight, now ready to return to cops and robbers.

'I go with?' she says, keeping a hand on the horse.

He sighs. 'Yeah, you go with.'

They mount up.

'Is this not how she was hurt?' inquires Abel.

'Yes.'

He nods with a rider's understanding and says no more. Abel's a horseman, a cowboy, a caballero. A courser had fallen on him once and broken his leg. He was back up before his doctor, who happened to be his father, gave him leave. Besides, the girl's riding with Sean. As they clear the stable and take a long, slow lap around the house, Abel's reminded that this man, this bizarre American, is one of the best riders he's ever seen. Might be he's never left his land, might be he doesn't know much, but Abel does know Sean is good and that the girl is safe.

And she's not felt safer for a long sight. Peaceful breeze on her face, gentle bounce of the horse underneath, ground rolling by as on a conveyor. That's when Emma starts with the tears. Doesn't last long. Wipes them away quick and grabs the reins from Sean and clicks her tongue and now they're at a trot and he smirks. She mutters nonstop in her language, prayers or what he can't tell. They ride up past the house along a flat at the top of the hill, down into a little gully then back up to the edge. Beyond is an endless country of hills, sweet and gentle, laid in near perfect patterns of brown and green. Flora swipes through them. Takes his ease, takes it all in, gestures his hand around like a page turning in the Bible, hoping Emma gets the message: take it in, girl. It's a gift.

They sit in this way for a time, idling as if they're waiting for the sun to hit its noon and nothing better's happening in the world. Good Heart's stoic in her pose, a regal wind blowing her mane, like she's given the air permission to touch her.

'There's a time when this was it,' he says. 'Just...me, the horse, the land. Used to be this was all that mattered. Mean to say, life was simple. It was nice, but a bit hollow.' She doesn't move. He keeps talking. 'Can't say when things changed, when I first started thinkin' about running. Then about settling down. Maybe all that heartache and strain was too much for me or the horse or the land. All kind of stuck together like a big block in me. This is back home, mind you...maybe that's why I ran. I tell you this, child. No matter where you go, no matter how long you stick with me, ain't nothing else going to feel like home. Call it a shit-heap o' sand, but it's still your home and it's still going to feel right. No matter if I take you all the way back to my own home,' takes a second to laugh, 'where the deer and the antelope play, nothing'll quite feel right besides that desert o' yours. I hope to God I never see it again...but I'd go back there for you.'

Whether she gets it or not she reaches back without turning her head, slaps him gently on the cheek and sighs. The moment will break soon and the hill will call them back and then the ranch and then Doña will laden the table with rice and beans and pollo rioja and the day will end and the future will be left undecided. But, Sean thinks, this earth is mine for a minute or two more, and thinks on which of these valleys can house his own place. Emma lays her head back on his chest and he smiles. Then the earth is back, belonging to no man. It was the first of many rides.

12. COPA

Next day comes without permission, like a long note on a cello disobeying its bow. Emma wakes up first. Curiosity's gotten the better of the girl so she rises as soon as she awakens, goes out to the hayloft where the helper-boys slept. They had all gone home night before, all except one. Ricardo'd spent the night in the loft and now he's up already. Emma hears him rustling in the barn, peers around the corner to see him leaning against the low partition of Good Heart's stall, chin resting on his arm. Other arms got something. A peppermint. Mutters to the horse in his language. Sounds even stranger than Sean's to her, even if it's more familiar. Stands there, waiting, then he turns and shouts and almost jumps out of his skin.

Emma laughs. Ricardo doesn't think it's very funny and says so in his language, speedily bumping over a number of curses and choice words. She doesn't understand and wouldn't care overmuch if she had. The Book didn't have too much to say on coarse speech and, either way, it never bothered her. Father'd had a tongue like a lash but had never used it on her. Just on the vagrant and tight-fisted. Now she's smiling and wondering what comes next. Ricardo grunts and stamps off, passing her roughly and flushing like a tub. Girl shrugs. She's patient, except when it comes to Good Heart. Trots over to see her and giggles and pats her snout.

'¡No la toques! Sólo le lavé!' Ricardo again, shaking his fist at her. Boy's well and truly pissed but somehow Emma just won't take him serious. Holds her hands up in mock submission and backs away, but her little grin won't go away.

Got a grin like an imp, thinks Ricardo. A pretty brown imp. Can't rightly stay mad at her, so he settles down, walks instead of stamps. Ricardo's not the sharpest, mother said so, but he knows Emma can't rightly understand him nor his two words of English: 'Food' and 'shit'. So, he tries the indirect approach and flourishes his last peppermint around like a prize in his left hand.

She at least feigns interest as he closes it in his hand, twists his wrists and makes the mint disappear. Unimpressed, she crosses her arms, but he's not done; pops his right hand open and there it is. Gives her a grin just for decoration and she's got manners enough to clap. He offers the mint; she doesn't take it. In fact, little girl's lost interest. Horse is a touch more fascinating at the moment, so she steps up to Good Heart and pats her on the nose. Horse nods and stamps, ready to play.

Boy's discouraged but he's a fighter; not the sharpest, but he can hang on until the bitter end. He joins in and pats Good Heart's flank and smiles and banters in a language she can't understand. Hopes his tone is right.

''Bout time for a ride, I think,' says a voice.

Emma nods and Ricardo turns to find Sean there, saddle and tack over his shoulder, proper cowboy's hat tipped low. Makes a menacing figure, a tall shade against the bright morning, or would if Emma didn't know better.

'¿Caballo listo?' he asks in Spanish.

Boy nods and waits expectantly. Sean knows the game and sends a little coin his way, takes a good long look at the beast, like a child feigning patience after he's unwrapped a new toy. Emma's never had a Christmas and goes to rip the saddle from his holding. He doesn't let go too easily but wants to see if she knows how to saddle this horse up by now, at least a little better than she did back at Castillos. She does. It's not perfect, needs a little fastening and the stirrups have to be lowered, but it's still uncanny. More than a girl who's only ridden a handful of times ought to know.

Feeling generous, he lets her take Good Heart while he borrows a speckled mare for his own. Thinks he's being generous anyway, like Good Heart wouldn't pick and choose who'd ride her.

'Se llama "Brillo",' says Ricardo, nodding at Sean's mount. He doesn't know that word but it sounds like a good name. They ride out together into the vast openness of the hills of Andalusia. A fearless void of grass, green and brown, and a sky like the ocean turned on her head. This is their peace. Here worries of strangers and cold death are run down by hooves, and tomorrow and all that comes with it is just a whisper on the wind, easier to ignore than leaves falling in autumn. Sean has most assuredly been ignoring it, too.

Brillo keeps her paces, not intimidated by the larger tobiano, but Good Heart's still the master. Unlike any horse he's ever seen, and he wonders why again.

There is plenty of time to wonder as they ride out like this every morning to stake claim to the land, whether or not it will be theirs, learning every hill and dell, little streams and shrubs and trees needing names. Days go by feeling like seconds in the wonder of the ride. It's pleasant: Doña and Abel are inquiring around looking for land, speaking to connections and local farmers for them while they enjoy the ranch and the land and the horses, even if things are still uneasy between them after his hasty return.

Emma pats him on the arm and points.

'What?'

She shushes him fiercely and he hears it too: a rustling in a dry band of trees ahead of them. Eyes narrow, hand moves toward his gunbelt. A snort issues from the trees, signaling the movements of an animal, not a man. Sean's still nervous. Emma grips his arm but releases just as soon.

She cries 'Copa!' with grand excitement, as if her dearest friend has popped by for a visit.

Yes, thinks Sean, Copa.

The sorrel stallion was docile as ever, crunching casually on some grass. Didn't look half bad for so much time on his own in this country.

'You look damn well,' Sean says, 'like you been brushed just days ago...well, more's the better. Let's get you back to the ranch.'

They mount back up and Sean leads Copa out from Brillo. Day's waning and they cut their tour short, heading back home. At the top of his favorite rise, Sean hears Emma shouting in her language. Remembers her English and says, 'Hey! Man! Look! Man!'

His heart sinks, a rock searching for the bottom of the sea. Strangers. Men with pale faces running them down. Can't tell who it is in the dust trail besides a figure, likely a man, on a black horse.

'Come on!' he shouts and grabs Good Heart by the reins, intending to lead her and keep Emma safe in the chase. Lasts about two seconds until the proud horse shakes her head and takes off back to the ranch at a gallop. Emma waves and he kicks Brillo and demands they catch up but they can't. Not quite. Copa's already huffing and neighing.

Dust cloud's far off and they'll beat it back to the ranch by a mile at least. He hopes Doña's got a gun. Mutters to himself now, each syllable matching a beat of his pounding heart; blue void's turned on him and frowns, gasconading its ruse.

Then the veil pulls back a tad.

Why? Why the fear? A man on a horse is nothing to be feared when the horizon's so wide. The world ends when you're dead, not in pain, not in fear. Fear's so real, though. It clings to him like a vampire bat. And it's her, not just the fear. Never has he had a little girl in his charge, someone else to mind. A man can handle himself when he's been halfway around the world and on his own for time out of mind, but put a child in the mix and none of that matters. All that matters is her and if there's a storm coming then by God he will be the lean-to.

Doña's shouting in Spanish now as he's almost ridden up on to the front porch and over Ricardo. Emma yells in her language and all is maddened noise until Abel shows up to bring some sense into the equation.

'We got a rider comin',' snaps Sean, 'Could be one of them was chasing us.'

Abel nods, disbelief a thin mask over his tanned face. 'As you say. Let's go and have a look.' He barks orders at Ricardo who bolts into the house and Emma trots after him. The two men stomp across the grounds in the direction Sean leads and they climb to the top of the barn by a rickety ladder that's not been in use for at least a few years. Dust cloud's there, much closer now, trailing a dark figure, foreboding to their circumspect eyes.

'¡Oye!' Ricardo tosses the rifle up to Abel and Sean marvels that nobody dropped it. It's a straight old thing, single shot and ugly as a gnarled oak.

'Thing work?' Sean looks pensive, nervous; his palms sweatier than his neck. Abel shrugs and grins that stupid grin of his.

Cloud's got a voice now. All they hear's the echo, an echo in the halls of perdition. Damned souls probably don't yell in Spanish, though. Rider's in white and black, waving an old hat and shouting. Words come through the echo.

'¡Americano! Donde esta el Americano?' He repeats.

Abel looks at Sean with youthful mischief in his eyes. 'That would be you.'

Ω

Priest doesn't look too well, like he hasn't been sleeping or shaving...or bathing for that matter. He munches down the bread thankfully, complimenting Doña at every possible moment, nodding his gratitude like he wants his head to tip off its neck. Sean can't help but wonder if his heart's still slamming in his chest.

He'd shown up terrified, babbling on like a Spanish locomotive with ruined brakes. Kept trying to see Good Heart, asking after the horse. Sean caught every fifth word.

Gently, tapping into that dusty bedside manner, Abel took the Priest by the shoulders and walked him inside the house. Ricardo and Emma took the old sorrel into the barn, the girl skipping gaily. After Priest calmed he started making sense. Came from town just that night after a scare, wouldn't say what, just gave Sean a dead man's stare. Then the food arrived.

'How'd you find us?' Sean asks.

Not a word, just that same stare. Abel even translates for him; still nothing. Takes a bite of bread and keeps staring. Then he decides, or something decides for him.

'By trying,' he says in Spanish. 'I was setting out from

town just last week when I spied Copa, who wandered up looking a little worse for wear. Castillo gave him a night of luxury and next day I took him off for a ride. You weren't too terribly difficult to track and Copa seemed to know the way, but the old fool bolted in the night as we rested on the top of a ridge!'

'You didn't stake him?'

'He is stronger than he seems! In any case, I could not find him and would not go the whole way on foot. Managed to get back to town with little trouble, got the young Arabian you saw, and found Copa's tracks. They led me to you.'

Another long pause and another munch of bread. Still hadn't answered why. Silently, he opens the satchel at his feet and fidgets with a cloth. Removes a large black book and puts it on the table. Black leather cover, remarkably clean with an odd shape etched on the front. Circle surrounded by ovular points, like teardrops, then strange little triangular wings bound to its sides. Sean doesn't like it. Reminds him too much of the flintlock he's keeping.

Emma, who'd been standing on a chair behind Sean, peeps over his shoulder. Doesn't like it much either, but it's familiar somehow. Her eyes narrow and she mutters something. Priest fires a very direct look her way and Sean likes that even less.

'We'll handle all this later,' he says. 'Padre's got to eat and there's work to be done here.'

Whether they agree or not, everybody disperses. Everybody but Ricardo who hangs around and watches the Priest, keeps him company and asks him questions about city life. From the doorway Doña crosses herself.

'You've got some explaining to do,' says Abel.

'Explained it already.' Sean looks him up and down,

squints in the afternoon sun. Emma trails after the two men as they march away from the house.

'Strange men? This is no way to explain a holy father come here with a book like that. Looks like the devil's Word!' Abel's not been to church since he was an altar boy but he crosses himself just the same. 'Santo de Dios…'

They stop. Sean assumes his thinking pose: hands on his hips, eyes cast down. 'I did a job, Abel. Down a ways across the Sea. Did a lot o' jobs, actually. Guy called "Jack".'

'Another American down in the damned desert?' Abel's tone rises up.

'No, he was local.' Looks at Emma for a hard moment, wonders if she needs to be dismissed. Kids were always dismissed when grown folks had strong talk back home. No, he thinks, this is just as much her problem as mine. If she can be bothered to sift through the language, then she should know.

'No,' he starts again, 'Local man. Real name's probably longer than my pant leg.' Abel blinks for the idiom. Sean keeps going. 'Nothing major. Just odd jobs as needed a good rider and someone didn't mind getting his hands dirty. Not like that! There was no killing. See…' Looks at Emma again. 'People down there keep to themselves. Those as want to be holy try to be, those as don't just stick to their lot. Jack had a hard time getting help for his operations, so when I stroll in out of nowhere looking for work he's praising Allah. Anyways…the last job was the hardest. Just about killed me. He gives me this thing and says, "Get rid of it. Put it in the bottom of the Sea. Don't look at it, just let us be rid of it."'

'And you looked.'

'Well, yes I looked! It was a…necklace or charm, talisman of some kind. Hell if I knew what it was, but I knew for sure it was worth a damn sight more than a trip to the bottom of the Mediterranean. So I kept it.'

Abel raises his eyebrows, expecting more.

'And that's it! I kept it. I went out into the desert, playing the part, and that was it. Very same day I get back to town to tell Jack it was done—'

'He believed you?'

'He believed it was off his hands and that was all that mattered to him. But it wasn't off his hands. Very same day things start happening in this town. Her father's killed. Jack's dead that night. We get chased out of town.'

'And all this is to do with some jewelry?'

Sean shrugs.

'Keep talking, Sean.'

He doesn't want to. Emma looks spooked and his heart is pounding. What in the world was he talking about, anyway? This is like some kind of fairy tale that don't look to end well. *Justice is only one-half done, though.*

'The man I killed, the stranger, was after that necklace... probably.'

'Probably?'

'Well, he killed Jack for it, wherever Jack got it. Killed her father, too, because...hell, I don't know why!' Then a thought struck him as hadn't before. 'Something to do with a gun he kept...maybe. When we crossed over, I did as I should have and threw it into the Sea. But the rest of them are after me now, for it and for my head.' Heart's racing, tears are coming, breath's running short. Terror. Night comes right in the middle of the day and the sun turns her back on the living. 'By God, Abel, they're coming for me. Oh Christ, why did I shoot him? They're coming, Abel. It ain't about no necklace anymore. I'm a dead man walking. They're coming for justice!'

That's about when he falls to his knees. Doesn't scream or weep, just holds his face in his hands and lets despair have its way, moaning all the while. No thoughts, just feelings and images. Home and death. Grief and despair, the unending void pulling him down with the crushing weight of the Sea. Man can't stem the tide forever and this tide rolls in hard, sweeping away all sandcastles of pretense and dried seaweed and hope, leaving only a drowning sensation.

But all tides roll back in time. They have to.

13. Despair

Takes him a good while to calm down. Emma's spooked to no end. Ricardo frantically tries his hand at reassurance, and it helps a little, but not enough. In the end it takes Priest to bring Sean back to the ground, and Sean does the same for Emma. He's her rock, seemingly, and when the rock shakes so does the footing. Gives her the right look, takes her hand, and they're OK again. Priest crosses himself and gives a silent benediction while Abel and Doña have it out, albeit quietly, in the kitchen.

She's telling him there's no way Sean can be left on his own. Something's happened; something odd and terrible and on his own he would surely fall to pieces. He reminds her that she's not his mother, that he's a grown man and if a man wants his own he can have it. Besides, the best plots he's found are no more than a few hours riding away from here. The mother hen can come clucking when she pleases. His winsome smile wins out, like it always does, and he gives her hand a squeeze, but behind the smile is a doctor worried for his patient. Like he's just found out a man's about to lose a limb, but he lies behind the smile and hopes it's the right thing to do.

Ω

Back outside, in the half-finished courtyard beyond the tile porch, he sits next to her under a tree in the gloaming light. They don't say much, can't say much because there's not much to say; more like bandaging and healing a cut in a few moments. It's him letting her know, though he don't know it himself, that he's there, that he won't be going anywhere if he can help it, that he's just getting started. And it's her, though she doesn't know it, trying to believe him. It's a strange man from a strange land, and a little girl from the desert, trying to weave the pieces together so they can be friends, so they can be father and daughter.

Let's let the last filaments of Day baptise us, he feels but doesn't think. Let the light of the Sun cover us and make us new and quench the fires of fear.

It's just a feeling, a feeling without words being no less real.

Priest ends this silent ceremony. Would've ended anyhow, as the final light slips away beyond the high ridges of the West. The pair of them look up at him and it's the same kindly old man who'd taken them in...except he's holding that book. He speaks strangely, in a language Sean's never heard, his tongue rolling and the words bouncing out as on a rough country road. It's not like the language here, in Spain, which rolls on and on, jerking and stopping, but rolling nonetheless. Not even close to his own language, slow and bumpy like a dry riverbed. It's new.

No, wait.

It's her language, Emma's. She looks surprised, taken aback to find herself understanding the sounds that come out of his mouth. Then she calms visibly, almost smiles, looks like a weight flies off of her. Priest even smiles, too, taking on the role of the comfortable Father again sitting in a pew, dosing a congregant with kind and understanding words. At long last he looks at Sean.

'I am Berber,' he says roughly, 'like her.'

'You just full of surprises, ain't you padre?'

Priest smiles and bows his head like a diplomat.

Sean sighs. 'Yeah, alright. Well, now that your tongue is loose you want to tell me what in hell is going on?'

'My English not so good, but I try.'

'Try then.'

Emma's fixated, smiling, delighted as if she'd just discovered a sweet in her pocket. But it's just one of her own, a child of the desert who, most importantly, spoke her civilized language.

But he speaks English now and what he says, the little of it she understands, doesn't do a thing to comfort her. 'When I am boy,' he begins, 'they tell stories that come from far. From Arab land. Story like about bad things, about...demon and angel and God and men. The stories for to scare little boy and girls to...be rightly, and work. When I am boy my father say me, "When you make a promise to a devil, it...,"' takes a moment to see if he knows the right word. Mutters something before he starts again. '"It never end,"' he finishes.

Creeping, unseen fingers grope Sean's neck, tingle his back. He wants to cry.

'After when you come church, I see man. Bad man. I do not spoke with him. I see him and I know,' points to his head to prove it, 'I know. And I look and I know more.' Breathing picks up, excitement builds. Priest can't stand it so he stands and hands the book to Sean, finger bookmarking a page. On that page is the amulet, the very same necklace Sean had been wearing up until he threw it in the Sea. The very same curious job Jack had sent him on. Now Jack is dead.

Priest's eyes glaze over with a sheen of tears and his mouth tightens and his moustache hides his lips. He crosses himself and gives the crucifix around his neck a kiss. 'I know,' he chokes and his English seems to flee him. 'I know.' And that's all that he can make his mouth do.

Silence. Silence that can fill a room. Luckily they're outside so the silence dissipates and flies away to rejoin the early night from which it came.

'What about Bibiana?' Sean's eyes are hard. 'They know about her?'

Priest shakes his head. 'No. She is safe. She I protect. You...you not so much.'

'Now just what in the hell does that mean?'

'It mean...' he stumbles again and looks pleadingly at Emma, says a few things in their language and she thinks for a moment and shakes her head. Then she perks up. 'Magic,' she says.

Sean laughs. 'Alright. Magic it is.' But he wants to see her, wants to know she's really out of harm's way instead of having to take the word of an old man who seems just a little crazier with every word he speaks. Mostly he just wants to see her. It will have to wait. Instead he sits, rests his arms on his knees and says nothing. He thinks nothing, says nothing, feels like his muscles weigh about twice as much as they should, like gravity just changed. Other two go on just fine. He can hear Emma gleefully chatting with Priest, thrilled to speak freely without interpreting the halting parade of languages spinning round her.

A moment later, or maybe hours, he wakes up. Legs are cramped, neck is sore from slouching. Still on the ground, still in the same place, but the stars are out in force and the crescent moon may as well be a frown. Priest offers him a hand up and he takes it, sucking air through his teeth and teetering on his feet.

'Now?'

'Now,' says Sean, 'I sleep...and we wait.'

Ω

Little breakdown took its toll but achieved a greater effect. Sean, for the time being anyway, is living unfazed, free from the heavy burden. Leastwhiles for now.

'Don't you want to ride out and look?' Abel asked over their morning eggs.

'No. They'll come or they won't. Right now alls I want is to have a look at that land.'

Abel had been talking it up for a few days. Nice span of acreage a widower's meant to put up for sale. Hills and valleys, good planting soil for grapes, nice house in need of minor repair and plenty of space for barns and pastures. Price was hefty, though. But what price was too much for a sliver of the Promised Land?

This is the next step, Sean thought. If I've invaders on my hands I need that Alamo from which to defend my own.

'You're not going to call it that, are you?' Abel voices his concerns.

Turns out Sean'd been thinking out loud. They're waiting now, out in one of the pastures. Emma's riding Good Heart, Priest is staring, Doña is watching them all from the window of her room.

'I don't know what was worse,' Abel puts as much cheek into his voice as can be mustered, 'Mexico, or the great American empire losing to Mexico.'

'Weren't America, it was Texas. Texas is full of boneheads.'

'Are you not from Texas?'

'No, by God! I'm from Tennessee. Leastways, I was born there and then I moved out west.'

'Oh. I thought all cowboys come from Texas.'

Sean wants to laugh but won't give Abel the satisfaction, leaves him to laugh at his own jokes.

'I missed you Abel. Can't imagine anyone I know using English like you, American or not.'

'I ever told you about the English family who come here on holiday?'

'Maybe you can tell me on the way. I want to see that land now.'

Abel nods and Sean calls Ricardo over. Points at Emma. 'We're gone for the day. She's in your charge, son. Keep an eye on her and the good Father.'

Ricardo nods determinedly even before Abel translates. Two men ride off, Sean lets his worries be trampled under hoof.

☊

The widower Herrera is an agitated man. Got to figure most men would be, losing a wife before her time, but Herrera seems even more so. Probably a crank before his wife ever opened death's door. Stands on the patio in the shade of early afternoon, a carven figure amidst the dun splendor of the hills. Black suit, as befits a widower, shaped ebony cane to lean on, thick beard and a balding scalp. The widower Herrera is huge, wide and tall. The widower Herrera is going on a long holiday, to the United States and to Mexico and to Argentina. He has no use for land or homes, for his traveler's trunk is now his home. The widower Herrera will live on room service and work handmaids and serving boys to death for the most meager of tips. The widower Herrera wishes to practice his English.

Sean learned all of this in the first minute of his time with Herrera. Hassle and poor manners, however, is of no concern for the stunning bit of turf and hills…and the expression on Abel's face, mischief and delight and disbelief, is worth the cost of admission.

'I am to go at week's end,' he says. Does his damndest to mask his accent and a fine job, too. 'I am wish to sell this land, but I am wish to make fair money. My hurry will be no…discount.'

The American raises his eyebrows and nods sagely at the last word. Can barely order dinner, much less haggle over land in Spanish, so the widower's a marvel. The outlay, on the other hand, needs some cutting.

'I won't quibble, Señor Herrera. But what you're asking is just a bit too high. Surely you can make the deal for nine hundred?'

Abel starts translating. The widower Herrera cuts him off with a stern raise of his hand and a nice, manly 'harumph'. He will not be rushed. So he takes his ease, though the tension's clear behind his jowl. Rests his hands on top of his cane and Sean notices the ivory pommel. Very nice indeed. The widower Herrera takes a long sniff of the sweet, southern air. Man could almost catch a whiff of the Sea so near. Salt and grass and wine and the very hills. Herrera would miss it, but not quite as much as he would miss his wife. It was time to go and leave the smells and the memories behind.

'To smell is closest to remember.' Sounds even more profound in broken English. Herrera eyes the two younger men in front of him, seeing if the meaning registers.

Abel bows his head, as if the benediction's just been given. Easy sell, making a big man feel bigger. Sean follows his lead and the widower Herrera, with seeming effort, removes his hand from the cane and holds it out. 'Nine hundreds.'

Bigger smile hadn't cleaved Sean's face all day, and he gives Herrera a big, American handshake—the kind one imagines in dime novels about cowboys who go out to fight Indians. Sean'd only met one Indian in his day, a Kickapoo named Lawrence who'd gone north after his people lost their land. He was the saddest man Sean had ever met.

Next hour is spent counting coins and surveying the land one more time, going over the house and the one or two issues that might actually need immediate addressing. Sean clucks and shakes his head, playing the part of the fool he was, handing over such a hefty sum to this shrewd man for land and a home that was surely worth less. In truth, he thought it a steal. Better to make the big man leave happy; everyone deserves that much.

It was about 2000 acres of good land, two valleys with good soil for the vineyard, plenty of grazing room for horses, a half-finished barn, more space than he'd ever need for paddocks. House needed a few new shingles and the privy would be better with some attention, few cracks in the walls easily mended. No, it was a steal. His piece; his own; his Alamo.

Stifles a laugh. When in hell did he ever want to be a rancher? When'd he ever want to make wine? After coming over here, likely, and seeing all Doña had and knowing a rolling stone can't end well and now he's got himself a ranch, all legal and proper. Well, mostly; Abel would sign all the papers as the only citizen between the two of them. But they kept a gentleman's agreement: if Sean ever let anything happen to the place, if ever Abel felt his name in jeopardy, he got a full year's harvest worth of wine. Now all it needs is a name.

'You can't name a ranch after a bloody horse!' Seems Abel's English improves with practice.

'I'm not saying I am, I'm just saying I might!'

Next comes a string of Spanish expletives that Sean can only half translate.

'Oh, what do you care anyways?'

'Is *my* ranch!'

'So I suppose you'll be the one to tend to the horses, and work out rent, and mind the vineyard workers, and keep up with the out buildings, all while dealing with your responsibilities to Doña?'

'Yes I damn will! If it means protecting my good name by not leaving you to name my ranch for a horse!'

They stop and Sean takes a moment before responding. 'Are you sure you want to do this? I can work something out with the magistrate and get the ranch in my name... probably.'

'No...no, it's okay. I just got...upset?'

'Upset sounds right.'

'Just don't name the ranch after the horse, please? Yes?'

Smiles and nods. 'Yes.'

Ω

The pair of them ride up to Doña's past the gloaming. First sight of happy lights in the windows, a tiny, gimp beacon among the hills, makes Sean's heart swell. For in his mind he imagines the time, very soon, when those lights will be his lights, and that home will be his home, and there will be a woman waiting inside and a little girl. Dreams the rest of the ride. Dreams of fried eggs in the morning and wine at night and horses in between. Dreams of Bibiana. Then clouds darken the edge of dreams and forces gather, strangers who come in the night, stalking patiently for justice.

'How you sleep in the saddle I do not know.'

Sean's eyes blink open. 'Just tired, I guess,' he murmurs.

'Herrera could make any man tired but me.' Abel stretches in the saddle, dismounts and leads his horse to the barn. Doña stands on the porch, looks disapproving as always. Tells them there's dinner inside, or what's left of it. Once they settle up with the horses and make it in, they see Ricardo and Emma sitting together by the fire. Priest's nowhere to be found.

'Gone a few hours now,' Abel repeats Doña's account. 'Just said, "Thank you", and rode off. Let him take Brillo and that Arabian and leave Copa.'

This makes Sean uneasy, not just because of the unfair horse-trade. Seems Padre either had divine business or something troubled his holy mind. Has to shake it off again, like so many other feelings. How much before the dam breaks again? Don't matter. He's got land now and a home. All he needs is a wife.

14. HOMEWARD

Wife's the hard part; ranching's the easy part. Spends the waiting week riding Good Heart (or Copa, when Emma's busy with the wonder-horse) around to various villas and ranches and farms, spreading word in his awful Spanish about his new place and asking if there are beasts for sale. Mentions the ideal land for grapes as well, hoping to get a stir and attract some of the local gents and experienced vintners to invest their time. Ideally he'd get some rich fellow to start a label and let the vineyards. Sean could sit back and enjoy the wine and let the land work for him.

Most of them say things like, 'That is well, sir, and I thank you,' but he's sure he hears things like *langosta* and *guiri* and *Americano* muttered behind his back. Time'll tell if they can smell a good deal when it wafts by on its way to the aether.

Emma and Ricardo pal around most of the time and Sean keeps his eye on them, wishing she'd pal around with Yessenia instead. Young girl, confused and traumatized, might be apt to do something stupid or run off with an overcharged boy. But she's happy. Riding better each day she's on top of that horse, and she's learning two languages at once. Joy radiates from her, or maybe the horse, when she rides; a star roaming over the hillocks and vales for small mortals to see and to marvel at. Sean sees it, wishes it was his, remembers a time when all there was was riding until life stepped in. No, until he stepped in the way of life. Stepped *on* it. One bad decision's all a man needs. Lord knows he's got more than one on his conscience.

About the time when they were meant to ride into town and meet the widower Herrera to hammer out all the legal matters and take the key, a very formal looking man with bifocals trips the alarm. Ricardo comes a'wailing into the house and Sean and Abel step onto the porch and see the dust cloud then make out a man in a suit on a brown stud. They make no moves.

'Buenos dias,' he lisps in perfect King's Spanish. He's come from the widower Herrera who's decided to start his illustrious tour of the world early. Tosses a satchel to Abel...not so much *to* him as *at* him. Inside are the final papers, two keys, and a handful of pesetas for their trouble. Abel looks at Sean. Sean shrugs. Messenger man waits patiently while Abel makes the decision that this is not a trap, and signs the paper and hands the satchel back to the rider. They don't invite him in for coffee.

'That's some kind of man.' Sean is annoyed but pleased. He's a landowner now.

'Well that...*capullo* is distraught. Just lost his wife. I guess we can forgive him. But I don't like this. Is not official.' Abel pauses and sighs. 'I should have read the paper better and ask more questions. I bet he's trying to...mess us around.'

And he's right. All kind of shenanigans have been done by better men; paper could've said anything. But Sean's too tired to worry anymore. He's ready to move and move on.

Evening comes. Sean is alone going through his things before the big pack-up and he notices that Priest left the book. That tome he'd brought along for the spreading of terror. Sean pauses a moment, wonders why he left it near that flintlock, and then cannot resist. Opens the book and shuffles through the odd pages in odd script until he sees It. The facsimile is damn near scary, like he'd dropped It in the book and not the water: a fine gold chain to fit about the neck, unremarkable, and a half-moon shaped pendant in the middle, swirling in endless design. Two smaller pendants to its side, each with their own lattice of unintelligible beauty. He had no wish to understand, and could not have anyway, what this thing meant and if it really even was the key to the riddle. It don't matter. Don't matter because Sean knows he's going to die, that all of this will be his end. He falls asleep staring at it and has no dreams.

Ω

A few days later they start the process of putting it all together: two bags, a small lockbox of gold, and the clothes on their backs. Doña is gracious and generous, though, and offers a parting gift or two. She smiles and pats him on the cheek. Her American son. He smiles back and goes in for a rare hug. The heaviness of the occasion, of life, slips away briefly and he is made free enough to show his affections. Then it's back to business as usual; mom's kept at arm's length and the world spins on and dark men linger on the horizon.

They step into the sun and visions of bustling activity open up. Ricardo runs along the yard with Copa chasing him; Emma puts yet another apple in the saddlebags and Good Heart doesn't so much as wince or blink; more of the stable boys are back this morning and Abel is there giving orders, calmly explaining this and that and how to shovel manure and how to stow the hay and what to feed the beasts.

Figure shoots past in a blur of blue and khaki; one more boy from town, called Jose, is late and his scolding is no more than a cold look and pat on the head from Abel.

'He's no slave driver,' Sean mutters.

When Doña looks at him he thinks of translating... but can't remember the word for slave. It'll come to him sooner or later, so he just shrugs wipes his nose and puts his hands on his hips and looks like he owns the place, as he will in just a day's time when he reaches his own place. But it's a place bought and paid for with blood money.

Thought it through a dozen times and there's what's right and what's right. Jack had no kin, no beneficiaries. They were scared and needing to run with no other means in sight. Putting the money into a bit of land's the right and honest thing to do. God only knows what Jack had intended for the funds.

Open an orphanage. Share with the church. Build a goddam school, says his brain.

Rubs his nose once more and stomps the poor feeling away. Emma rides up on Good Heart and says, in damn near perfect English, 'Good Hearts ams rowdy today!'

Man can only laugh. 'Best to show her what's what and who's boss, girl. Run it out of her.' Takes his hat and swats and the hindside of the wonderful beast, who takes his meaning and trots off before she kicks into a slow gallop. Girl's a real prodigy, too, he notes. Also notes Doña staring at her.

Sean'd given Emma the book some days ago. Girl might've been able to cipher something out of it, surely she could read her own tongue. She'd said nothing as yet. Likely she just forgot about the whole thing, but it's in their bags all the same.

'Pues,' Abel's walking up towards them now. 'Time for you to go and make me a proud ranch owner?'

'Just about, I reckon. Not like there's too much to bring. Though Doña here's passed along a few parting gifts.'

'Copa?'

'Copa.'

Abel grins like a wolf. Doña had claimed Copa since the Priest had run off with Brillo. Clearly the old stallion wasn't worth the trouble to her.

'If Copa were a person he would be drunk all the time. No act of charity giving her to you.'

Doña says something scornful.

'*And* she is giving you a bed? That is surely something.'

'Very kind of you, Doña. Gracias!'

Woman just pats him on the cheek again.

Even kind enough to give them a waggon to carry it all in. Copa gets that job, but the sorrel doesn't seem to mind. Spend the rest of the bright afternoon filling it up with the bed, now disassembled, their miserly bags, and whatever odds-and-ends Doña feels nostalgic enough to part with.

'No, uno mas,' she says, tapping a finger against her mouth in pensive thought. Then the woman barks at Jose or one of the other boys to run somewhere and get something. Boys make games of such things, shouting and laughing as the graying monster speaks their names. Dart off to the barn or the house or the stalls or the yard. When the game ends Sean and Emma win: several stacks of hay and feed, a few tools, a chair or two, flour and maise, even a saddle and tack.

'Doña, muchas de esos va a estar en el nuevo—'

She shushes Sean before he can finish. Just wants to feel like she's a part, like she has something to give. 'Let me do something for you',she says in Spanish.

It's the doing that stalls them. They aren't off until the middle afternoon, which makes Sean uncomfortable; he wanted to be off early to possibly make it home by sundown. All the same, today's the day. So they hitch up the cart to Copa, who looks like he'd rather be under a bottle somewhere, and Sean drives. A little assemblage sees them off: Doña and Abel and Jose and Ricardo and Yessenia and some of the other boys and girls from the ranch stand in a long line and wave. Sean tips his hat, says something about seeing someone another day, and clicks Copa into motion. Emma waves and blows a kiss to Ricardo and Abel laughs and thanks God Sean didn't see it. Smiling like an imp, she rides ahead until Sean calls her back. Kids chase after them as kids do, just as the horses and cart pick up speed along a path barely visible, bearing them north to fortune and, maybe, a new start.

They chat along the way, best they can, best as any father and daughter of only some weeks could have done. That is, they chat when Sean isn't occupied by thoughts of Bibiana.

'What's the story on that Ricardo?' he asks as menacingly as he can.

'Ricardo?' She laughs a gruff, musical laugh; a harp played by a cactus.

Stifles his own laugh and keeps playing the part of Angry Dad. 'Yes, Ricardo!'

'Ricardo is funny boy. He...' she waves her hand vaguely. 'I like.'

'Like. What do you like about him?' Just makes out

her eyes squinting in the fading sunlight so he drags her along. 'He makes you laugh?' Sean gestures from his throat, helping her along.

She nods, 'Yes, yes. He very divertido.'

'You like being around him?' At great peril he nudges Copa and the waggon closer to Good Heart to make his point. 'Near him?'

'Si, yes.'

There's a pause like a cow ready to give birth and he says, 'Do you love him?' and realizes how stupid it sounds out loud. She's thirteen years old, fourteen at most. But girls back home been known to marry just a few years older...

The girl looks serious and clicks Good Heart ahead at a canter and Sean has to stifle the instinct to shout at her, make her come back. Does so on her own a few minutes later, pulls alongside Sean and looks him up and down.

'No. I no love Ricardo.'

'Sorry,' he murmurs. They don't speak the rest of the way.

Ω

Takes them all evening long. Night's quiet, more quiet than Sean ever thought a night could be. No birds, no chirping critters, just the wind. The lovely, quiet wind. Lets the ease and the peace wash over his aching heart. Lets the *clop* of the horses, the creaking of the waggon, the faint harmonic rustle of the grass fill the void, endless and foreboding above him. But even the void is not void. There are stars there, light beyond all light; a moment even shadowy terror can't touch.

Christ, what am I going to do? he asks himself again. And, again, no answers come save one, and it is the worst answer: wait. When a man's used to running, waiting feels like the most horrible thing to do. To wait is to die. And maybe that's just it: he will wait to die.

No! That won't do. And again the civil war in his mind reaches a ceasefire and again his thoughts turn to Bibiana.

Emma's asleep in the saddle, a trick Sean had barely mastered after riding thirty years. Girl's got to be part angel or part ghost or something, he thinks. No, best not to say such things.

They begin their ascent of a low hill, and when they clear the rise Sean can barely make out a house at the edge of sight, illuminated by the sickle moon. He whistles and Emma starts, says something in her language and pinches her cheeks. But the sight of the house excites her. She shouts and when she moves like she's going to kick Good Heart to full gallop Sean shouts back.

'Together,' he says.

Emma nods while her groggy brain sorts things out. 'Together.'

So together they go, at the same slow trot they've been going at all evening. House gets bigger, horses huff a little more at the end of their long journey. And like that the dream begins.

They stop at the porch, stake the horses and unload some bags, toss them at the door, stretch their legs, look around. Emma runs and peers into the windows and screams and jumps back. Catches her in his arms and shouts.

'Man! In! Man in house home!' she screams and his heart takes off like a bird fluttering away from a gunshot. She's right: two beady eyes stare back blurred through the window. The pair of them jump back and Sean immediately moves for the saddlebags, going directly for the revolver, that fine piece of devilry stolen from a very devil. Five shots left.

His fears have come to fruit sooner than he thought, but the sooner the better: shoot another one down and be done with it. Demon, sorcerer, or just a fool stalker, matters little. Pivots and points, both feet planted firmly on the ground, both hands on the grip, two fingers on the trigger, two thumbs on the hammer.

'¡Oye! Que es el Padre! Que soy yo!'

Sean blinks and the Priest is standing there before him.

'It's I! In the name of God, is me! No shoot!' Poor soul must've crossed himself a double-dozen times and now he mutters and sputters in Arabic. Grips his chest and Emma rushes at him, shoves him right in the ribs so he skitters aside and now she's wagging a finger and waving her arms and yelling all manner of things in all manner of languages.

'Ya homaar! Idiota! You...you...tozz fiik!' and she caps it all off with a growl to make her father cringe and all is quiet. Sean closes his eyes, draws a ragged breath, almost feels his lungs shudder. Gun goes away, sleeve goes over his face. It's nowhere near hot outside, but his blood boils and now the only sound around is their breath desperately trying to catch up.

'What the hell, preach?'

Priest pauses, bites his lip. 'I am sorry. It...I am very sorry. I no want scare you.'

'What are you even doing here? How do you know where we live now?'

He wants to smile but that might be the worse thing he could do. 'Well...news is fast, you see. I hear in town a... Norteamericano buy Herrera house and he already talk... it must to be you, yes?'

Sean nods a nod of annoyance.

'So, I am here. To see you and how you are. I wait but

I grow tired of sun and...well, I am sorry but I try the door. Is open.'

More disappointment. Damn Herrera didn't even lock the door.

The Priest peers over Sean's shoulder, eyeing Good Heart. 'I sleep and...here you come.'

'Right. Well you can help us unload.' Steps between the Priest and Good Heart and tosses a bag at his head. The old gentleman catches it before contact is made. Man can at least get a little work done. 'Get some lights going, too. And a fire.'

So they unload as much as they can. Herrera's been kind and left a good deal of furniture. Extra bed comes in handy as Emma gets her own room. Priest can get a fire going in no time, so soon the wide ranch house is warmer than it needs to be in late summer, but it's cozy and bright all the same. All lit up, the house is quaint on the inside: white walls, brown tile floor, wooden furniture arranged haphazardly. Sean'll want to bring in some order but it's a fine home, finer than he'd thought when he first saw the place. Finer without the widower Herrera around. Likes the wooden ceiling beams in particular.

When they all settle in it's late, but they chat all the same. Emma enjoys being able to talk plainly with someone in her language, even if it means Sean is the one supposed to be quiet. But Priest keeps saying how he wanted to check in on them, make sure they were okay. Keeps staring long and hard at one, then the other. Then he talks more about Good Heart. Even goes out to the barn to see her.

'All right, preach?' asks Sean.

Man nods and forces a smile but there's a low, smouldering ember of concern behind his eyes. His mouth quivers. 'Bibiana ask after you. She help me with the English little and when I tell her I come for see she ask for you.'

Sean smiles. 'Well, as you can see we're okay.'

'Okay only? Why no go and for to see her?'

Sean thinks hard on that. Why not? And why not soon? It's all he wants to do, after all. 'I've only just got here, haven't I?' But that's no excuse, he thinks. Like she hasn't been on your mind since you fled that town, says an alien voice, a sweeping tingle through his shoulders, neck, and skull. She's a fine woman, it says, and if there's so much as a chance of a spark, well then you'd better tell Copa to get over himself, get back on that horse and shove off. Go and see her. Sweep her off her feet and bring her back here and make a life. Patchwork life, but a life nonetheless.

He sees Priest staring at him. Emma's nodding in her chair. The smoulder's become more of a twinkle.

'Maybe I'll go and see her,' Sean says.

'Yes. Of course. Now, I can be here for the night? It is late.'

'Yes, fine! You...yeah,' Sean smiles. 'Thanks for asking.'

Priest continues to stare and stare at him as Emma sleeps peacefully. He stares and words escape his mouth that Sean cannot understand and the room grows cold and then warm again and he smells something like clean earth.

And then Sean is far away. A man is there, odd-looking, felted. He wears a black mantle over his felt black coat, black feathers protrude from under his white hat, as if his hair were a raven's wing. A hand glides slowly and a book falls down and disintegrates before it touches the earth. Mouth moves soundlessly and his teeth, cracked and brown, dance up and down and he passes the hand before his face and what was once a rocky waterfall dries and is a sand-waste.

Now he, if it is Sean, rises above the sand and chases

the horizon but the light does not change. Leagues and miles he goes, flying over the empty dunes, his speed increasing with the force of his will. But the setting sun keeps moving just beyond his grasp in unending twilight. He hears something. Below him, now, is a rushing, small watercourse. Starts in the middle of the desert and runs its straight, now winding, now straight way to the Sea. Sean follows. It twinkles in the light and joins its twinkling with the flickering waves of its Sea. And into the Sea he goes, free. Such freedom as he has not felt in waking life. The freedom the imaginings of his countrymen attribute only to the eagle. The freedom of an infant, now walking. But the freedom chokes him. And as the answer, a lost meaning that promises a forever of truth, claws its way through the murky saltwater, past fish and weed, his vision goes red and he can't breath and the red turns black.

15. WAITING

The sun is in his face. He is awake with contracted lungs. Awake in his own home, white walls bright in the morning sun. Emma. Where is Emma?

'Hullo, you!' says a girl's voice. Emma practically skips into his vision, pride trailing off her, holding a cup. 'Cafe!' she exclaims. Sean, bewildered and disoriented, takes it and the girl runs off again. He's not sure he's ever said 'No' to coffee before. Sips it and it tastes horrible and he wonders how this girl helped run a hostel and never learned to make a proper cup of coffee.

Runs a hand over his mouth. 'You like the house, I take it?'

'Oh yes!' she calls from somewhere he cannot see.

Then he remembers something like he probably should've remembered a while ago.

'Where is the Priest?'

'Padre? He go...no to sleeping.'

The man exhales and nods and rubs his eyes. What had he been dreaming of? Tries but he can't recall. Can't matter much. Dreams are odd things best left to doctors and palm readers. Still, though, this one felt important somehow. But it's like trying to recall an evening after its sixth shot of whisky. Few things are more difficult. It had something to do with the Priest. Priest. The book.

'Emma, you ever read that book I gave you? The black one?'

'Oh yes.'

'Well?'

'Eh?'

'What do you make of it? What's it say?'

'Is...um, baby book,' she says, her voice less muffled as she moves about the house.

Sean's taken aback more than a step.

'Yes. Baby book,' she says. 'For baby.'

'What?'

'Is baby book.'

'Yeah I got that. How do you know?'

'Padre...no Padre, my padre. He say stories of that me.'

Just like that the object of his fears are dismissed by a child.

'You'll have to tell me some of these stories—'

Two arms close about his neck and cause the coffee to spill. Emma gleefully hugs him, pressing her face against his and making a sound like she's just tasted the finest cake man can find and now he's a father again somehow and he has a home to manage and a girl to help.

'I tell you story!' she says.

And yet beautiful fatherhood cannot distract the bell in mind, chiming for Her.

Next few days are a pleasant blur amid the endless blur that is life on the run. They rearrange things, eat quietly, tend to the horses. All is just a kindly time of getting used to new surroundings. End of the first day, and the place is starting to look more to Sean's liking: orderly, clean, everything in its place. It's calming and thoughtful work, and so all the while he is distracted by something. Emma is daring with her English, chatting almost nonstop, only to receive 'Hmmmms' and 'Yups' in reply.

End of the second day, he comes out with what's been on his mind: 'Get packed, girl. We're off tomorrow.'

☊

Emma's annoyed. All she's hoped for over the last month is home; one better than the one she'd had, where her father had died. A new home to make new the life of a daughter, to forget what had happened. Her wish was to leave the table and the bloodied floor behind, cut it away from her mind like the rotten protrusion it was.

It was all in her grasp, too; new house, barn, horses to look after, and a man to look after her. Two days she'd had of her paradise, of her new life in the world. Two days and now she is riding behind Sean, cursing the back of his neck for all its redness and stiffness. Copa is a slow horse, slow and stupid and lazy. Not caring or too burdened to. Not like Good Heart, who is free and loves her freedom and cares about every blade of grass her feet trample. He's riding her and he knows how to ride her well and look after her, but she is not his horse. Two days and now she is going back to Doña and Abel and that tiny house. Back to Ricardo. Even that, however, isn't enough to stall the great *harumph* she looses for the God-knows-how-manyeth time that morning.

'Dammit, you're staying with *Doña*!' He practically screams the last word. Patience died about a league ago. Girl doesn't like it but it's the only way; can't leave a young kid alone on a ranch in the middle of the hills. And she can't go with him, she'd just get in the way. Got to stay in the only safe place he can think of. So, it's back to Doña's.

Rest of the ride is dull and tense and the hills seem to roll under them. It's leisurely riding, the worst kind of riding. Emma lets all this happen unhappily, thinking of tricks to play on Sean for vengeance's sake.

Even an old cowboy like Sean gets tired of having his rump in the saddle all afternoon. He's grateful for having a proper hat as the sun makes no move to tip its hand: just sits there blankly, sliding across the sky. Pair of them pass the same little streams as they'd crossed days ago but Emma's not quite over the thrill; loves the green land the way she loves Good Heart. Both are free and soft. The desert is free, but coarse; too coarse for her liking now that she's been to greener places. But the desert, unflagging remnant as it is, is strong in a way that the green isn't.

'Give up on my ranch so soon?' says Abel with a wide, devilish grin.

Emma'd been daydreaming. They're already here. Abel'd ridden out to meet them. Dreams do have their uses, then. Better to be dreaming than angry on the unending road.

Sean laughs and smiles. 'Just getting started!'

The last mile or so Sean explains things, how he's got to go back to town and Emma'd best stay here and that Doña and Ricardo'd look after her.

'And what is so important at the town?'

'Business.'

'Business. That is very funny.'

'You ever operated a ranch, young Abel?' Doesn't mask the annoyance in his voice.

'I work at one most of my life! You know this!' Abel pushes the words out between laughs.

'Yeah, *work*. Work for Doña or Dionisio! Running one's different.'

'I see.' And then there's a lull while Abel looks like the cat who ate the canary. 'And how is she going to help you run things?'

Sean squirms in his saddle, staring out, pretending the horizon's a puzzle that needs figuring out. 'She?'

Abel laughs so hard that Emma, starting to understand what the two men are talking about, thinks he's going to choke.

They leave it at that. Such is their understanding: an older brother and a younger, one always out to chide the other as hard as possible in that odd, manly affect.

Upon arriving at Doña's, the sun seems to yawn to prove how lazy the day is; Ricardo is asleep on the porch but Doña, the ever-industrious, is whacking a rug strung up on a line. Dust scatters into the breeze.

Sean has no wish to explain things to Doña, and he knows poor old Abel will end up in that hated seat before the day's through, so he tips his hat, nudges Good Heart next to Emma and pats her on the cheek. 'I'll be back in a day or two, little girl,' he says and smiles. She hugs his neck.

☊

The long ride to town gives Sean an open place for his thoughts to swim. Just a man and his horse and great brown and green hills. Thinks of Bibiana a lot, but he's got no earthly idea how he's going to pull this one off.

'Buenos dias, Bibiana,' he says to the countryside. 'Marry me? Marry me, mi amor? That's stupid. That's why English and Spanish don't go together.'

Good Heart grunts in agreement.

'Quiet you,' he says. Horse-talk's an easy habit to fall into when a horse is all a man's got to speak with. Especially a man who prefers to talk when no one's around, like Sean. Ground starts to rise, hills get steep, Good Heart don't mind a bit.

'Honesty, I expect,' he continues. 'Woman like that requires honesty and a sincere look in one's eye.' Then an old, sad feeling comes upon him, one he doesn't even want voiced in front of Good Heart. Feeling's like, *how can an honest woman dare to be in the sight of a rat like me?* Sometimes, he thinks, I must have just been born to bring trouble alongside with me. Bad trouble and she'll die.

More silence then.

Day wears away easily, slowly, like a burning candle undisturbed by wind or breath. That steep incline that had given them trouble on the way is trod down, a blink in a day full of them. At the top, though, the hills give a fine view of the country, of town and the Sea beyond, a vast strip of blue at the edge of sight. All there is between Sean and love (or foolishness) is green grass and a couple of shrubs. Somehow he wishes there was more cover between him and that woman.

Even in the dim gloaming he can spot Castillo's ranch far off to his left. Town, though it's composed of low buildings and one tall church steeple, seems to loom before him as a white giant with brown hair, peering straight down and piercing his heart.

'Pete's sake,' he mutters, 'You'd think I was wandering into the belly of the beast.'

The hairs on his neck crinkle and the quiet is pulled away in an instant. Three riders, galloping hard, fly past him. Three dark clouds against the dark of dusk flying past like a gale. Sean starts and puts a hand to his hip. They pass not three feet from him, two on his right and one on his left. And as soon as they come they go, not stopping or turning their heads, cloaks blowing and whipping with the tails of their horses as they penetrate town limits and disappear. Didn't even hear them coming.

Sean's got to take a moment, collect himself, scold himself for his distraction. That could have been it, old timer, he thinks. Even this fair country has bandits...and worse. Shakes his head and kicks Good Heart, who didn't so much as whicker, and they're for town. Still, the hairs on his neck won't sit down.

Good Heart eases into civilization, hoofs clatter on the cobblestone. She's the most confident beast Sean's ever known. They pass the church. He takes a different side street, meaning to avoid Bibiana's house. Even in the dark can't take the risk, not until he's more presentable. So he skirts the house, at least two streets away, and rounds the bend into the thoroughfare of town proper. It's quiet, not lively like the frontier towns of his youth. No drunken chatter, piano music, whores on balconies. Just one or two walkers and a few lights from which misty shadows could be seen. Finds the inn easily. Tallest building in town, at two stories, and twice as wide.

Innkeep's kind but wary, looking the *guiri* sideways as he strolls in so late with his horse lashed to the front porch.

'Uno cuarto, por favor,' he says with no hint of an attempt at an accent. But, he can pay and that's what counts. Sean uses the bathhouse to tidy up. Time he's ready, clean and in cleaner clothes, it's late, past 10 according to the clock in the foyer. Guess he'll have to call on his lady love the next day.

Tomorrow seems like a long ways away, and an hour after he puts head to pillow he's grateful there's no clock in his tiny room. It's not the grand hotel, just a quaint little room with bad art on the white walls and an oil lamp and a bed. Should be just the thing to settle the mind and get one to sleep, but his mind's all muck. Not even real thoughts, just images, flashes attached to anxiety, a chill up his spine, worry gnawing at his skull. His will is enough to keep words out of them, images are still there until night-shadows gobble them up. Creaking floorboards and scratches at windows and doors. Puddles of ink bleed through them and become terror and fear and righteous justice. And then he wakes up.

Ω

'No me gusto lo,' she says, though it's more like a mutter of a whisper.

Somehow Abel always ends up here, this soggy ground between Doña and her fears. She's a worrier, a mother to none and many, a widow and a businesswoman. Times like these are when Abel's most apt to agree with his father, that women probably shouldn't run ranches or any business for that matter. But his father was a classic man, a man of the past. Abel is one of the present and future. Tries to comfort her and let her know it's alright, but he might as well be telling the sun not to set.

'You worry too much,' he says in Spanish.

'You always say that and you're always wrong. I worried about Sean when he went away and look at him. He's a mess.'

'So you're prophesying now, *mami*, and not just fretting?'

Doesn't have much to say to that.

'Let him go through his time. Let him do this and then we will see what we will see, if he stays with the ranch or goes back home.' That's what he says but his heart doesn't believe it.

Doña looks at him coldly. 'He won't go home.'

'No?' He takes another sip of wine. 'Why do you think he can hardly speak Spanish or why he always looks like he's a thousand miles away? Because he *is* a thousand miles away, across that sea in America!'

'Don't shout at me.' Tries to show how calm she is, but she just seems more frightened.

'You are just afraid, Doña.'

'Damn right I am. I've been afraid for you, for Ricardo, most of all for Sean. It's like God put him in my charge those years ago. Who's ever heard of that? An American stumbling into a horse farm in Spain looking for work! That's crazy talk. But he was here, he came to us. And now he's left and leaving again.'

Abel's never been a very spiritual man, but he makes the attempt all the same. Anything to quiet her down: 'Maybe it's time for you to let him go, give him back to the Lord.'

She shakes her head but she doesn't say anything at first. 'You just don't understand me. You've never understood me—'

'Don't! Do not! This is not about us! This is about you and Sean and your motherly fears.'

Quiet shames him, or at least she means for it to. Learned to take that slug years ago

Abel exhales. Got no patience for the woman but can never seem to break away from her. Maybe he's the kind of man that always needs a woman and if there's no spouse to be had and no mother, well, then this is it. She takes his arm, looping hers around it. It's not a comfortable place but it's the best that they have when all they have, for now anyway, is each other.

16. Resolution

Should've had more than just coffee, but he wasn't in the mood for magdalenas and somehow his feet won't take him to her.

By God, am I a little boy again trying to talk to a girl at the school house? Apparently so.

Takes him half an hour to get properly dressed, get the shoes tied, and get out the damn door. Hands are practically shaking, so he goes walking. Out the door of the inn and right, away from her place and towards nowheres. No, he thinks, towards the Sea.

Early enough so the town's half-awake. Stalls half-empty, windows half-shut, walkers half asleep as they go wherever it is the day demands they go. All the while the gulls shriek and the sweet stink of sea-air accompanies them from here to there. No boats today on the rocky coast. Sean clears the dusty streets and the murmur of the town's waking day, stumbles out to the long stone formations that create the harbor.

Sheer cliffs to his left. Hadn't noticed those before. Black and brown and green and beautiful. But his real destination is the Sea and the spray, and the salty air says he's there. To what end and purpose? For the Sea is black and barren, even in the early light of day. He stops at the edge of the pier and looks, but there's nothing to be seen.

Heard, though, is something different.

He hears it. What it is he can't be so sure, but he hears it under the gentle waves and lapping water, the gurgling deep. A watery voice or the whisper of it, just there beyond the edge of hearing. Winds tug at his hat and jacket. Thinks of that dream just two nights ago and shoves it away, harshly, wonders if this life of his is dragging him under. Wonders if being dragged under's so bad, if the taint and shadow of his inner man could be washed away with water and, if so, he can find the peace and happiness he once knew. Before the mining camps and cow towns and the world left their mark on his soul.

Sean Denman blinks and sets his jaw and marches back into town past barkers and children playing and cider vendors and shops barely open for business. Stomps past it all and goes straight to her house. No resolution, only grim determination.

He bangs on the door. Bangs again. And again. She's not home.

Sean sighs a sigh to blow the door down. No budging. Taps his foot, does all the gestures one does when he's frustrated and trying to hide it and express it at the same time. The church! Of course she's got to be at the church. Jogs this time, determination changing and lightening as something else butts in. Trots across the street to the wide double doors of the church that's not too big and not too small and opens them and goes inside and she's there, kneeling.

Can't cut in on the Lord and ask for a lunch date, so he waits. Sits quietly in the back, thinking nothing and saying nothing. Never did take a good look at the old church, but it's nice. Small, neatly arranged pews, images on the walls and candelabras flanking the chancel. Wooden altar's towards the front, more candles, and golden (Gold-plated, he thinks) ceiling over the apse. In it a man can marvel at the Lord if he doesn't feel like speaking to Him, or any of his saintly bannermen. Then he cracks a smile, remembering a cowboy's prayer he'd heard somewhere.

Lord, I've never lived where churches grow. I love creation better as it stood, he thought, and before he could get to the part about being buried and living open to the stars, Bibiana is there standing in front of him. Woman doesn't say much, or anything for that matter, and Sean shoots up to his feet like one of those stars he was just thinking of. It isn't a good start.

'Lo Bibiana, ma'am.' He says it reflexively and tips his hat reflexively and he hates himself. Hates himself, that is, until the smile breaks loose on her face.

'Hello, Mr. Denman,' says she, and immediately he's transported away to music and flight. In the short weeks away he'd forgotten just how desirable her accent is. 'You look well. And I like your suit!'

He laughs at that. Takes his time just looking at her, takes his hat in his hands. If she's a lady, then he ought to at least try to be half a gentleman.

'Thank you. You look...well, you look lovely as always.' Got to bask in the warmth of her smile, take his time, let his heart slow up a bit. Then the words just come. 'Can we sit a moment?'

She may have said 'yes' but before he knows it they're seated in the pew, turned towards each other and then the awkwardness comes. What to say next?

'How's padre? He back there?' Points behind the altar and to the left.

'Oh, no. He's away. He did not say where he was going, but I presume it is parish business.'

Odd. Man should've been back yesterday at latest from

Sean's house. Was that yesterday? Of course it was. Oh well, he thinks, parish business.

'English lessons still going well?'

'Oh yes,' her steely calm belies a fluttering heart beneath her dress. 'One student's gone away. Her father's a sailor and she had to go with him to Africa. But the rest remain. It's a living.' She shrugs and smiles.

'Well, I think you speak more fairly than I remember.'

She nods like a sage. 'And Emma? Good Heart?'

His turn to smile now. 'Both well and thick as thieves. That girl may know more of horses than me already. Hard to say what she'll do next. English is even moving along and I don't doubt that she knows a thing or two in Spanish.' Cheeks almost hurt for smiling. 'Good Heart's still the wonder horse, by God...' Smiles to cover his coarse speech here in the house of the Lord. 'Both fine. And you ought to come and see them. That's really why I came here. But why don't we walk? We'll get you, you know, a basket. Some food. Find a place to eat.'

'I think the word you are looking for is *picnic*.'

He laughs again. 'Same in Spanish, innit?'

'Just about.'

'Just about.' He stands and offers his hand and is more than pleased when she takes it and they move towards the door and their heels clack and echo.

'Damn!' She says without hesitation. Sean's eyes go wide. 'I have a lesson today.' Seems to fret but only for a moment. Easy smile creeps back on her face, saving his hopes from dashing. She shrugs. 'They can wait. It will be my first absence from class!'

'I hope to make it worth your while, then!'

'Me too.' Can't tell if she's kidding, nor can she, but they walk out together and she takes his arm like a lady and they walk in the sun of noon through the shade of the small buildings and over the rocks and grass to the market. They make a basket, as perfect as it is simple, and many who watched them thought they saw two lovers of many years still delighting in the freshness of a spring they knew together long ago. They stroll beyond town, northwards, and there they find something like a glen and take their ease in the shade of a tree. Talking, mostly, eating a little, resting and lounging. The awkward feelings come and go, and they share more than they'd shared with another man or woman, or any human, for a long spell.

Sean dodged specifics, but told her of his time in America: growing up in orphanages and escaping like many other a boy who'd lost all to the Brother's War; eaking out a life on the prairie; the long and loathsome journey across the Sea to Spain. She told him of a life in near paradise, quiet but not untouched by grief; the sweeping changes in her country barely felt here along the coast; a husband taken when he was just barely known. They spoke easily, marveling but barely feeling the passing of the day. And it remained the finest afternoon either of them remembered for a long while.

$$\Omega$$

Arm in arm they walk to her steps and to her door, setting sun off aways to their right. Sean feels good. Can't remember the last time he courted a woman, and never one so lovely as Bibiana. Only misstep was an adventurous mistake, shouting 'Come on!' and grinning like a buffoon and dragging her down an alley, small and dark, on their walk back. It was a boy's mistake, impetuousness for the excitement of the day. Two men, rough sailors by the look, stood at the end, paying them no heed.

'Maybe we'll go back the other way,' he'd said. Bibiana nodded her agreement.

So besides getting over eager and nearly stumbling into a fight, he thinks it was a good day. Perhaps the best day. If he wasn't already in love, he is now and now he's there with her and they're stepping up onto her patio and her hand falls into his.

'Thank you, Sean, for a fine day. I knew you were a gentleman when I first saw you.'

'Well,' now he's all grins. 'I was hoping the day wasn't over. There's something I got to talk to you about. May I...may I come in?'

She feels her heart lurch, for more reasons than one, and feels herself smile and nod without a word. They step in and sit in the small parlour.

'I don't really have much prepared. I could make some coffee, or...'

He's holding her hand.

'Just, lets just sit down. Okay?' Sounds serious, nervous, scared. And he is scared. Because somewhere under his thoughts are evil men riding against the wind, raiding and killing and stringing him up by his guts. And by God, he's dragging her into whatever godforsaken mess he's put Emma and Abel and Doña in. But that's just a feeling under his thoughts. The mind can't reckon with such things as fear presents and he feels such love in his heart as not to care. His mind must be clear for what he's about to say and so he lets the fear be and calls it nerves.

'I,' starts again, 'I enjoyed being with you today, Bibiana. It's the kind of day I've wanted since I saw you. And I think...I don't think it's the kind of day I can be without again.'

Her expression, tight from the fear in his voice, softens to caution.

'Just, I just want you to listen,' he says. Now she's nearing amusement. 'I want...every day to be like today. I've got a ranch...sort of. Anyway, I have a ranch and I have Emma but I need a woman to fill out the space. I mean. That's not what I mean. I mean,' now he's almost laughing. 'I need you, Bibiana. I want you around.'

She smiles. 'Do you know, I have only ever been proposed to one other time in my life? The first one was much better than this.'

First he's hurt. Then angry. Why would she say that? Put his heart on the line and she's going to kick it?

'...And he courted me for a month with flowers and bica gallega and wine...'

But the tone in her voice tells him something and he lets the hurt go. Not far, though.

'...and I feel sure that he had a ring of some kind...'

That's when he wants to jump in, explain that he'll get the biggest ring she's ever seen, that the ranch will pay for everything. That this needn't be the proposal, that it wasn't meant to be...

'...but, somehow, I like this proposal. Were my father alive he'd call you a gringo and show you out. God rest his soul, he did not care for the English or Americans...'

About his turn to laugh. Her good humour, though, belies the fear in her belly. She's wringing her hands.

'...and I have always wanted a cowboy of my own.'

He grins and chuckles, stands to dust himself off, then does the biggest, grandest bow man has ever known, sweeping his hat all the way down to the dusty tile floor. 'At your service, ma'am. Now and for always,' he says. 'And there's time enough for a proper proposal.'

She squeezes his hand and lets him pull her up and press his lips against hers.

Ω

Bibiana sits on her bed, elated but with a weight upon her. She'd thought of Sean often, more often than she'd want to admit. Tried her best to chalk it up to girlish fancy, but then he came back and she knew the feelings were true. An excitement lined with fright and joy and uncertainty. Their time together ended just as splendidly as it had begun. Sean had been a perfect gentleman, leaving her with a kiss and an embrace and the promise that he'd return as soon as the sun rose.

But ghosts accompany her. The men in her life that had come and gone. Her father looked down upon her, her husband wept in the corner. Father Orellana was not there in her imagination and she wondered why. Priest had never judged her, only loved her as a spiritual father.

The fight's the same as ever, a repeat since the day she met Sean and the same as any time some man had passed through town and stoked her imagination. The ghosts wrestled her down and kept her there in her tiny house and her English lessons and her closed life. She had prayed to Christ for release and freedom, to the Holy Spirit for peace, to the Ever-virgin Mother of God for strength, but they were slow in their arrival. Perhaps Sean was the answer to this prayer, but if she stayed, kept the 'Yes' she had said without saying tonight, then he was on the firing line.

No, she said to herself. It will not be like the last time. Antonio had put himself in harm's way and been killed for his foolish beliefs.

It was nothing to do with her. But she was still angry at him for leaving, for choosing his beliefs over her, for leaving her with a gnashing fear to keep her from caring again. For caring could only end in hurt.

'Damn you!' she says aloud. And then screams it. And then, skin crawling, she paces and pulls her hair and prays for release, for freedom to choose, to love Sean as she wishes to. But the tangled wrestling resumes.

I don't love him, I love the idea of him. I do love him, it's my broken heart that makes it so hard.

The fight is not worth it, the struggle too much. It's all too much. There is only this tiny life in this tiny house and then death.

And when she collapses onto the bed, the release she has prayed for comes and she cries sweet tears, tears she wished she could bottle and keep around her neck to remember as a relic. And like that it is over. It would not be over forever, but in that moment her mind and heart were as one, together in purpose and hope for the future. She would not renege, she would keep this man as her own and let him keep her. Takes a racking breath and wipes her face and lays there in the quiet, sleeping some and waking, until morning comes.

$$\Omega$$

He wakes up in his bed at the inn alone, but it's the finest alone he's ever felt. No hangover, no shame or regret. The only other presence is simple joy; excitement to see her again and make today like yesterday. Up he gets and out and down the street to go to the church first. Priest is still not there. Crosses the street and bangs on the door. She's there and all grins and he says, 'Come with me. I want to show you.' Thinks twice and says, 'Better pack something, too.'

By some miracle or other she laughs and holds up a small

bag. He sees she's already in a riding dress as well. By God, he thinks, and she's grabbed his hand and dragged him around back and there's her horse saddled up. Laughing and whooping he races back to the inn and scrounges up Good Heart, saddles her faster than anything ever done, and shoots back to Her like an arrow from the string and she's still there, by God, waiting atop that night-black of hers and he can't help it but canters up, takes her by the waist and kisses her once more. She blushes and shoves him away with a smile and kicks the horse and they're off.

'Wrong way!' he calls in glee and she turns to follow him with a joyful laugh and they're over the hill with the Sea to their backs and home ahead.

17. Happiness

Some two months later is the day. Would've been one month had he had his way but, things being what they were, sometimes an extra month is required.

'About time to open this stand,' he says to the sky, surveying the *Good Heart* ranch. Don't look much different than when it was bought, but it looks good, tidier somehow, like a proper ranch with the white adobe house, the barn, and best of all the wide open range. *El Rancho del Corazon Bueno* did not have quite the same simple, grounded feel as the English but it would do. When in Rome...or Spain, as it were...

Speak of the very beast, Emma rides down from the hills upon her, trots over to Sean and nods her oversized hat at him like the little ranch hand she's become. This has been her habit, her morning ritual, waking up Good Heart (she imagines), setting saddle and tack, riding over hilltops, and singing to the grass, or whatever it was she did. Girl and horse were near wed and Sean had long before admitted to a touch of jealousy.

'It's time?' she asks.

Nods back. 'Yes, ma'am. Now why don't you get ready and act like it is?'

She frowns, clicks, and sends Good Heart around the fenced vineyard, the first acre ready to receive the workers. Canters past and into the large barn where Good Heart and Copa make their home. Soon enough the place'll be full of beasts, and those as are willing to pay to have their beasts trained up proper.

Hell, he thinks, I suppose I ought to be making ready myself. Gives the kindly, warm ranch house one more approving look. It is a fine place. Makes a mental note to thank Abel once more, perhaps with a bottle of wine. Moves back into the house and as the door shuts, out of earshot and vision, horsemen overtake the horizon.

They come in twos, then threes, heads covered from the hot sun, horses stumbling weary in a clopping line, dust seeping up from the dry grass underhoof. The gang descends the low hill towards the ranch with coarse purpose, and as they do so crests a large waggon carrying their necessities. Minutes later they engulf and surround the ranch.

Sean struggles to button his shirt like a child. His fingers fumble over each other and he mutters curses, fear and anxiety thumping their way over his nerves. The loathsome buttons only push him harder. The day is important, but not so much as to set a man back to infancy. Then there are footsteps on the hard floor, a creaking of the door, and he starts with a gasp. Emma is there staring at him with a look that says, What is the matter with you?

He wonders the same thing, almost looks pained, then she walks in confidently wearing a soft, plain white dress. Smiles and helps him to button. Scratches his scruff, the everpresent shadow of growth on his cheek, like another animal on the ranch to tend to. 'No shave?' she inquires.

Before his smiling mouth can form a reply there's a

crash outside. Loudish. Unexpected. Emma looks out the window and murmurs, 'They're here.'

Rushes to the front door and out. Sun catches his eyes before they do. No hat today. Eyes focus and there they are: half a dozen in black, shadows looming with doom.

'Y'all are early,' says Sean.

The first woman holds out her hands and shrugs. They unload the waggon, pulling out posts and white cloths and the like.

Well, he thinks, they're here to help make today beautiful.

But beautiful is nothing without Her and she is not here yet. Be here soon enough, he reckons. Until then he can wrangle these decorators. Such folk, though, are harder to herd than cattle. Minds of their own, even between each other, and no clear direction to the end result. So it's all a man can do to cluck here and there like a hen and shout, 'That one goes there! Aca! Aqui! Aya!' whilst trying to button his shirt.

And then like a bird from the clouds she's there, radiant in splendor and joy. Doesn't see her at first; too occupied with the help. She slinks up with mischief on her face and taps his shoulder. He turns, breathes like a bellows catching fire, and grins thinking heaven's come down. Because it has. He takes its hand.

'Where I come from, it's bad luck to see the bride before the ceremony.'

'Where I come from, you pray for luck. Brides don't make it go away.'

And then they just smile as if the world is paused and time has turned aside.

Ω

Last few months have been good. He rides out to see her in town; she rides to see the ranch. Emma comes, sometimes Ricardo or Abel, but it's always the two of them. Doña would not come, not before the wedding. There was talk. The more talking there was the more sure the two felt of each other, of their place. That dawdling fear and darkness at the rim of Sean's mind blurred and folded, if it didn't run away completely. Only thing as reminded him of it was the other her: Emma. Seeing her would take him back to the waste, some times; to mud houses and dead faces.

Bibiana herself weren't troubled by such thoughts. The dead faces of her past were melting in the beams of happiness and expectations. After that great day, she was nervous and told Father Orellana as much. He smiled in his fatherly way and listened and said, 'Come back in a week.' Week's time had the nervousness cracked and peeling and underneath was excitement. Excitement grew and blossomed each time Sean came to town and she found herself staring out the window, waiting for him in anticipation; each time she saw his face peering out the window of the ranch likewise.

But riding was the thing, almost always. Riding out for picnics and to see the land and even faraway towns where the Sea lived as an afterthought and dark riders never tread. Old feelings came back to Bibiana sometimes, that is until something shifted on one of those journeys, midway down a low mountain. It was like a shawl which, nudged by the wind, flitted above her eyes to show clear the path for a fleeting second. And she said nothing. She smiled, breathed, reigned in tears and gripped Sean's hand a horse away. Naught more than a feeling, joy and grief and great happiness all ordained. Peace, we would call it. Another foretaste like the one she'd had in her tiny house.

And had there been a doubt in her mind, returned from the void, it went away. The rind of nervousness flitted away completely. This bizarre union they'd set in motion was to be. He corrupted her English, she beat him with Spanish; he taught her to ride properly, she taught him fine food and the way to treat wine as wine and not whiskey.

Ω

And then the joyous day arrived. She'd come early, taken to an empty room in the ranch house and waited. Now she'd get back and find a way into a white dress, lace over her shoulders and down her arms and a veil long enough to lead to the Sea. Padre would do the words, Emma would be the maid of honor, Abel the best man, Doña the one to weep in the back.

All arrayed like heaven's angels now, each one is in their place save the bride. No guests save a few of the boys from Doña's house and two of Bibiana's English students. Decorators did a fine job: the space between the house and the barn is overhung with white banners and flowers, little altar made of wood and white tablecloth at the front with the holy cup. White hangings on either side turn the work-worn buildings into a proper setting, fit for the proper Catholic wedding Bibiana wanted. The tree that lives between the two buildings, old and near death and bearing Sean's scorn, had been kept despite his protestations and now serves as the centerpiece.

Priest arrives, finally, looking haggard and in need of shave. Smiles, though, and hard and doesn't stink of booze. Sean's not sure why he expected that. Shakes his hand, Priest gestures over the setup, smiling and lauding.

'It will be a great day!' he proclaims, though it feels forced somehow.

Now made ready, the meagre crowd stands in the hot sun. Sean exhales a storm and runs a hand through his hair and tries not to fidget too much. Sure as he is, he remains nervous as any man would, but the thoughts and feelings pass through and over him and he, too, is made ready. Emma now rounds the house, the very picture of white joy, the dress contrasting her complexion, her green eyes smiling wider than her little mouth. She winks at Sean and takes her place and he's distracted for the briefest of moments and then She comes.

Her feet round the house first, the vanguard, the white flag of peace; in a blink she is striding down the aisle, a vision of beauty; in another she's beside him, smiling, a happy tear in the corner of her eye. Sean would remember none of the words, though Priest said them; would not remember every line on her face, every crook of her mouth; would not remember the sacrament or the birds or the sunshine. He would remember, and only after deliberation, a feeling of weightlessness, of floating above the dry ground, and of feeling, for once, absolutely happy.

18. Wine

Establishing a marriage, and a household, is not a small feat. Man has contended with the notion, and failed, since the beginning. Snakes and apples were involved. Man and woman from different lands and walks should make the process all the more challenging, and yet the two are doing okay. Fights are common but so is forgiveness. They get by, most especially so as ranching duties can take a man's mind off a quarrel as would otherwise drag him down for the better part of a day. Having the man out of the house for many hours will clear a woman's mind as well. So will the long ride to town for an English lesson or a proper church service.

Emma gets by, too. Matter of fact she flourishes. She rides every day, speaking Spanish; rests every night, speaking English. She learns to read, to paint, to cook Spanish food from her adopted mother.

'Ponlo ahi!' she would shout. That calm, saintly demeanor often left Bibiana in the kitchen. If cooking was an art, then it was a performance art and Bibiana would stop the show.

Abel, Doña, and company are the perfect neighbors: many miles away. When company's desired they show up, when it's not they are too far away to be a bother. They would laugh and carry on, Abel often complaining in half jokes that his investment is squandered. The man refused to change, saw nothing apart from his joviality, only wanted to ride and keep the boys of the ranch in line. Probably never left so he could inherit Doña's place and make a little empire of himself, or perhaps he really believed he had something to give to those boys. And to Doña.

When Sean would inquire into his future, Abel'd say things like, 'I am but a young man! My prospects ought to be squared away before I go courting, a lesson you never learned!'

'I ain't so young,' Sean would reply.

A strange tension between Doña and Bibiana came in waves and often in the kitchen, most frequently when the recipe was brought into question. It was the most polite infighting Sean'd ever seen or heard of, though the Spanish was so rapid that he only caught half the conversation. Was it mother protecting her stolen son? The queen facing dethronement? Or the kindling of friendship being stoked to a blaze?

Ricardo often came with them, and often Sean would look upon his coming with distaste. He was brash, an irritant, a horsefly that paid no heed to whipping tails. He talked too much and much too often to Emma, and he was a terrible flirt and he knew it. Abel would laugh and Sean would scowl at the way they talked and held hands.

Many evenings are spent under the stars, thinking and talking about the future, a future full of horses and wine. The vintners came. Some weeks after the wedding, a man arrived at the ranch unannounced. Moment Sean realized a stranger was at his door his heart leapt up into his throat and he dove for his pistol, nearly scared the soul out of

Bibiana and, sweating with fear, peered out of the window
to see it was no more than a well-dressed man patiently
waiting atop his mount in the yard. Hadn't felt fear like
that in some time and the shadows appeared again and
Bibiana asked and he wouldn't say for fear of sounding
like a madman.

'No secrets between us,' she said.

'I know,' he replied. 'Soon.'

He stepped outside and gauged the look of the man:
fifties and thoroughly mustachioed with an interpreter at
his side. Introduced himself as Felipe Ayala. Name meant
nothing to Sean, but he'd later learn that the man owned
three of the largest vineyards in Andalusia.

'Mr. Denman,' he said through the impeccably polite
interpreter, 'when I heard of a small ranch with much land
run by an American looking for aid in making a vineyard,
I could not help myself but to come and see this wonder
for myself. By your leave, I will inspect your land and then
present my offer.'

Stunned to silence, and grateful for the lack of pretense,
Sean nodded and wondered if angels or devils were looking
after him for such things to land in his lap. When they
rode away, he quickly readied Good Heart and trotted after
them, Emma scowling from behind; she was just about
to begin her morning ride. Instead she marched back to
the porch and enfolded herself in the arms of Bibiana,
watching the riders vacate.

Ayala pressed his fingers into the ground of the plots,
scooped up dirt and sniffed it. Sean swore he saw the man
taste it, though the moustache served as good camouflage.
He frowned and fiddled with his hat, rode back to the
ranch and took coffee in the yard with the rest of the
household. Bibiana made as fine a hostess as Sean could

have wished, creating an officiality to the little business that would have otherwise been absent.

Ayala had not spoken the entire ride, nor did he speak when coffee was served, nor did he speak for an hour after he'd finished his cup. Finally, when Sean thought he'd burst, the vintner nodded a greatly rehearsed nod at the interpreter. Emma worked to keep from laughing at the eccentric old man.

'Mr. Denman,' began the automaton, 'your land is not all it could be, hardly fit for the growth of grapes. In time, though, I can make the land worthy of my name.'

Sean flushed and Emma broke with a hearty laugh.

'I will offer you thirty percent of the take for each harvest, though we cannot expect to sell the wine for some years, you understand.'

Sean sniffed, thought of Abel, and said, 'Forty.'

There was a lull after the interpreter conveyed the new number and looked at his employer who nodded like a king signaling the start of an execution.

'We are agreed then.'

They stood, shook hands, and that was it: Ayala and his interpreter rode off into the sun, leaving Sean wondering if this had been an elaborate dream from which he would soon wake. Emma put her index finger above her lip, then two fingers to make the moustache even bigger, and puckered her lips. Bibiana laughed and that was the end of it.

Many evenings are spent in worry. Sean's wariness returns. Many days he rides to Doña's place under the guise of wishing to see his dear old employer and talk about purchasing more horses for the ranch, but in truth he is fearful and the fear will not leave him. Riding and seeing for himself that his friends are not dead stave it off, but only so much. It is a single trestle trying to hold up a bridge doomed to fall, for he knows in his bones that death is coming.

He thumbs through the black book that the Priest left him, Emma's 'baby book', understanding none of it, fearing and hating it, taking no comfort in the disturbing pictures of demons and travelers and kings and courtesans and animals. Keeps it to himself, hidden in one of the barns where none should find it along with the ancient gun Emma had handed him in a village at the edge of the Sahara. Bibiana would often question him. 'Soon,' was always the answer.

Horses are purchased. One from Doña, a charade of a deal meant mostly as cover for Sean's endless intrusions. One from another rancher and two more from town. Old Castillo has a happy hand in many of the deals, serving as reference along with Bibiana for the *Americano*. Handicap as his nationality may be, it also proves a fine wind to push along news of his ranch. Such territory belongs to true *vacalleros*, and the thought of an American running a horse farm here was a mystery at best. It is no tourist destination, but farmers come to draft horses, other ranchers to talk horses and discuss studs and breeding and suchlike. It damn near starts to resemble a community and Sean, Bibiana, and Emma start to look like a family.

� ♺

That family grows when the time comes to breed Good Heart. Those local ranchers had come a'courting as soon as word spread and they got a good look at the tobiano. Any man who knew horses could spot the potential in her a mile off; talk of linebreeding and brags on well-to-do studs come in like rain for months and Sean shrugs them off, hard and fast. Started to feel like marriage proposals and he's almost as protective of Good Heart as he is of Emma. Decision had to come to a head and it does at dinner one night.

'You know, old Castillo says that Abano's got quite the stock,' began Bibiana.

Sean doesn't look up from his rice. 'You don't say.'

'Indeed. I spoke with him in town today.'

Emma taps her fork on her plate thoughtfully. 'You think Good Heart want babies?'

Sean looks up at Bibiana. He wants to know, too.

Woman shrugs. 'Who can say? Seems natural, though, even if Good Heart isn't quite natural.'

'Now just what does that mean?' says Sean.

'She's just the brightest, smartest horse I believe anyone has seen. Castillo says so and you're always raving about her.'

Sean only chews quietly.

'I think she like babies. What you say "baby horse"?'

'Baby horse is called a "foal", darling,' starts Sean, greedily grabbing onto a comfortable subject. 'Boys are "colts", girls are "fillies". And I don't think Good Heart is no dam.' Goes back to eating and mutters, 'And no sire's good enough for her.'

Bibiana nearly laughs at her husband, but her face turns thoughtful instead. 'Even a wonder horse won't live forever. I think I should like to have her around longer in her children.'

Emma nods enthusiastically. She is no stranger to death, and knowing Good Heart could live on in progeny is an exciting thought. Sean only chews, not unlike the horses in question. In his mind it is decided: Good Heart is too good a damn horse not to breed, even if he doesn't like it, but he doesn't have to let his family know he'd caved so quickly.

$$\Omega$$

Most evenings are spent under the stars. Sean and Emma speak of horses and he tells her tales of the West as he knew it, as he understands it to be now. Mostly of horses, though, and how they are the West, really. How they are the land and how they make one honest. Even Indian stories he'd heard passed around, about ponies of course, tell the same. It's such things as unite the father and daughter. Oftentimes Sean finds himself preoccupied, wondering if it's the only thing that unites them. It was obvious that the addition of Bibiana into the equation had yielded jealousy on his part. The two got along so well, and he so busy with the ranch, there were times when he felt secondhand. But in the nighttime they speak and he feels close to her and it's on such a night that Sean asks a question, one that had nagged him only because it hadn't come up before. Almost feels ashamed by it.

'What's your name, darlin'?' he asks out of nowhere. They're alone. Bibiana's inside.

Emma looks at him and looks away plainly, like she did all that time ago when he found her. Like she still doesn't understand him.

'Little girl.' It's a bit firmer this time. 'What is your name?'

Looks at him again, sips from the cup of water, and waits. It's the only name she has, the only one that fits her new life. All others are skin shed in the desert of another world. The name is who she is now, as fitting and bound to her as Good Heart is to the horse they love so well.

'Emma,' she says, and curls up in her chair.

Ω

Few weeks later is when the day comes for Good Heart. Doesn't need to look twice at Abano's sire to know he's a fine damn horse, a tall black Mallorquin, almost as rare as Good Heart. Abano, a tall man himself, grins broadly at Sean's reaction to his finest stallion. In the yard the two horses sniff and prance about almost immediately.

'Dios mio!' exclaims Abano. 'We had better make some kind of arrangement before these two couple without our parental consent!' He smiles again, though the joke is mostly lost on Sean and his stubbornly poor Spanish. Wants to talk about estrous cycles and breeding jargon to distract from the looming fear, but he doesn't. He's still hesitant, even though everything feels right. Not quite ready to kiss Good Heart and leave her at the altar even though Priest had had a long talk with him days before.

Ω

Father Orellana had come out of nowhere, as was his wont, seeming calmer somehow, far calmer than Sean had seen him since the day they'd barged into his life. They sat down for coffee and he wore a smile. Sean felt wary but the day was good: cool and sunny and breezy. Emma hugged his neck.

'I have try to help you,' he said in English, 'as good as I can. I think I fail, but I have one last thing for you. Let Good Heart breed. You will wish it to be so. She must go on.'

'Bib put you up to this?'

'Is this important?' the older man leaned in seriously, furtively though there was no one else present. 'You know what is to come, or you think you do. I believe you must let the horse go on and so save Emma...and yourself.'

Sean gripped the chair but masked the seriousness on his face. 'What do you know about what's to come? You've done nothing but meddle and sow fear and give me riddles.'

'There is nothing I know, only what I believe. In the name of God, for you and for Emma and so for Bibiana, let the horse go on.'

The conversation ended in a stare, the priest's eyes glistening before it stopped. He stood, said his goodbyes, and left an hour later. they had not seen him since. Nor would they again.

Ω

Bibiana elbows him in the arm and smiles warmly and kindly. Emma watches Good Heart and her suitor from a tree branch nearer the barn, as excited as she is nervous.

'Yeah, alright,' he says at last, not bothering to even try a word of Spanish. Holding out his hand is enough and Abano takes it and Bibiana prattles off some niceties, filling in for her silent husband. They would leave the loving couple alone for some days, time enough for them to sniff more and let nature put them through their paces and eventually mate. In a year, or so they hope, a beautiful foal would be joining them.

Ω

Most evenings are spent outside watching the Sun go down and the Moon come up and the stars alight. Looking up at stars and Moon, Bibiana asks her husband in a voice bringing finality with it: 'Tell me why you are afraid, my love.'

She takes his hand, to comfort him and keep him close. But he doesn't want to be close, wants to squirm away

[189]

and hide his shame and confusion and be left alone with his secret far from the light of day. Doesn't even have to look at his wife to know this has to come out, that now's the time.

'Back aways over the sea,' he begins. 'Where I met Emma we...crossed paths with some men before we met you.' The words are forced out, half-muttered and slurred by tension. 'I believe they killed her father. Killed my friend. Chased us out of town and approached us and I killed one of them. Last saw them on the coast but they're feeling's stuck with me, always haunting the edge of my sight. They're in every stranger, every rider, every dark night.'

Stops then and wonders. Why not tell her about Good Heart, where she came from? His wife's soft eyes speak concern and sympathy and fear, ready to receive more.

'I remember the day we met, the fear on you. I know what it's like to lose a life but I can't imagine what it is to take one.'

'It was self-defense!' he cries. 'I'd no choice in it!'

She strokes his arm, breathes to keep her heart calm. 'I know. I know you, Sean Denman. You're not a killer.'

'Yeah...it's just...Hell, I feel like I've been stuck in this without my knowing it. Without my doing. God knows I'm no saint, but I feel His wrath upon me. Had no choice! He was coming at me! I shot him and I put him down and...and I took his horse...'

Bibiana's face is stone until her lips move. 'You mean...'

'Yeah, I mean!' Pump's primed now. For every word of truth he speaks a wave of lies crashes against it. Wounds in his heart are torn fresh, but fresh for the healing. 'I know they're coming! I try to do right! I've more than I deserve. You make me decent, Bibiana. I'm not a good man but you make me decent. You love me, don't you? Now that your husband is a killer and a horse-thief?'

She sits up and addresses the fear in his eyes calmly. 'I do love you, Sean. And you are a good man.' Can't say why but she leaves it be. Says nothing else but strokes his hand again and turns her head away.

19. MUD PONY

Sharing the truth with his wife, even the little that he did, had been a balm. Mind felt smoother, days felt lighter, heart didn't feel cramped and twisted half the time and the months passed in a steady rhythm befitting those as have found their calling. Life was horses and food and a day's work, one at a time.

Ricardo'd come by more often and Emma'd sneak off with him when she was sure none were watching. Couldn't take horses, as that would be too obvious, but they found a grove of trees in running distance at the bottom of a hill a mile away. There they'd sit and chat in awkward fashion, thinking about what the other was thinking and hoping it was about them. It often was and it was often innocent, their lollygagging and idle speech in English and Spanish and words only they knew.

He asks her when she will come to him, to Doña's, back to his home village and see his family. There is so much for him to show her! She has only seen a tiny part of this country. There are churches and castles to see; towns upon high hills of stone; sloping vineyards from which come the finest of wines; even wider, grander valleys for Good Heart to run free in. Or so it sounds to him. To her, it is the half-understood dream of a wild boy. But she likes to hear it, likes his dirty face patched with wisps of a beard to come. Likes the way he's kind to her. Even learned some

English, some phrases in her language.

He tries again with his paralytic English. She shushes him. She tells him of her land, of the desert, how it is wretched and wonderful and hot and dreamy. How she will take him there when they are older, when she is ready and when things slow down at the ranch. Sounds like a dream to him, too, what he understands. Believes it more than she does, takes it with urgency the way young men do. Impetuous and eager, but she makes him patient.

They decide quiet is best. Hours scamper by. Their ways part. She walks back to the ranch in the early light of morning, the predawn of a new day, and Sean sits on the porch. Perhaps it was the mellowing of marriage, or marriage to a holy woman of irremovable patience. Maybe it was the settling of his spirit into the earth of an actual home, but Sean did not attack. He brooded and stewed, but his voice was measured and calm.

'Where you been?'

Stunned silence.

'Where did you go, Emma?'

'You know,' she says.

'No I goddam don't,' he says with the same measured patience. 'I know damn well *who* you were with, but what I don't know is where in the world you two run off to.'

Fear is rising like a dark cloud over and between them. Old fear that Sean covers himself with like a worn blanket, an old friend.

'Just away, down the hill, not far. Not unsafe.'

'Unsafe is that skinny brat. You know he's older than you, yeah? You know what he wants.'

'He wants love! To love me!'

'Hell. Don't matter what he wants, matters is you staying close. Staying home. God knows what's out there!

Jesus!'

'Nothing! Nothing out here! Is only trees and grass and hills!'

'You don't know that.'

'*You* don't know that! You are 'fraid! You are...*cobarde!*'

Sean rises from his chair on the porch. Hears Bibiana scuffling in the house. Patience stays in the chair. 'Did he say that?'

'No, I! I say that—'

Hears the gunshot a full second before he sees the blood spattering out of Emma's side. The child's eyes go wide as saucers, awe and pain. Sean feels his heart go up and down at once, up to his throat and down to his stomach like a bitter stone. Without thinking he rushes to her, spouting curses as she collapses to the ground, her knees unable to brace her agin the shock, and he scoops her up and now Bibiana's out of the house and he's yelling 'Get in the fucking house!' and she's gasping and dashing back inside and he's right behind her. Lays her on the table, looks at the wound with shaking hand and ragged breath and thanks God the slug seems to have only pierced her side clean. She's pale though, scared near to death and shaking.

'Blankets, now!' and Bibiana complies with shuddering whimpers and quiet tears and he presses the fabric to her side, hoping to stop the bleeding. 'Christ, we need Abel. *Christ!*' he shouts and she starts. Rummages through his mind, thinking of what Abel would do.

'Water!' and Bibiana gets the pitcher and they wash wound and Emma's crying softly. Okay, okay, he thinks, wound's not so bad. Think it missed her guts, think we just need to stop the bleeding. Okay, okay...

'Sean!' a voice calls from outside. 'Sean,' it says again, 'time to talk.'

Bibiana's eyes go wide as her gaping maw. She starts to shake.

The voice is American. An American accent, western-like as Sean had heard through every cow town he'd ever set foot in. His stomach is water, his veins icy as the Missouri before thaw, only the ice is crumbling. He's falling apart.

'Just...hey...just, keep pressing down...' he stammers to Bibiana. 'Darling, just...hold the blanket like that. Yeah?'

His wife says nothing, eyes pleading, hand holding the fabric, breath coming too quickly.

'Maybe...Jesus, maybe you can sneak out the back? Go and find Abel? No...' eyes dart like a terrified rabbit. 'No...'

Walks off like he's half-dead, a shambling wraith in dark houses. Hand on the doorknob. Outside. Three riders standing in a row in the morning sun, hands in fingerless gloves, dangling over their holsters, faces shaded by wide-brimmed hats, scarves over their mouths, long dusters and leather coats and dirty shirts.

Christ! he curses himself. Hell! Why've I left the guns? What is wrong with me? You're afraid, Denman. Dead afraid.

'Hello, Sean.' Can't tell which one is speaking. 'Figure'd it was about time we had our little talk.' One in the middle sweeps off his hat, holds it in his hands. His head is bald, pale as cold sand, painted over one side. Maybe this is the speaker.

'Killed one of our own, you did. And stole what was ours.'

Sean licks his lips and blurts, 'Why now? Why not last year? Why not last month?'

'Reckoned the time was right. Seems your affairs are in order.' All three shifty eyes glance at the house. Cheeks raise under veils. They're smiling. Sean nods slowly.

'So, Sean, we can make this all right. All we need is for you to come with us.'

'Only gonna kill me soon as we're done doing whatever it is we're doing. You'll kill my family, too. Already shot my *daughter*!'

It laughs. 'Your daughter, eh? Little desert rats don't belong here. Little desert girls belong in the desert, especially those with fathers who think they're demon hunters. Anyways...you're right. We are going to kill you. One way or the other. What you stole is awful important, but not so much as killing one of our own, however you managed it. How did you, anyway?'

Sean's silent, tension grows with the heat of the day.

An impatient growl from behind one of the masks and then, as one, all three step forward towards Sean and there's a bursting at the barn and a galloping of hooves and another gunshot. Good Heart tears past the riders, who turn and begin shouting and wailing, then one tumbles over, shot in the shoulder. Bibiana's on the porch, nearly drops the rifle she's just fired. One of the strangers races down the hill after Good Heart while the other two, the one shot rising slowly, return their attention to the house but Sean's already back inside. They're calling in unintelligible tongues, sounds of grief and rage. He bars the door, locks it; bars the other door once Bibiana falls inside.

'Upstairs!' He glances about. Where is Emma? he thinks and then a gunshot breaks his concentration. Straight through the window and over his head. Bibiana shouts and crouches at the stairs and fires back and the stranger in the window doesn't move, doesn't so much as blink, but stops his shooting if only for a moment.

'Upstairs!' she calls and he races ahead and grabs her by the arm and drags her up the wooden stairway and is grateful he taught her how to shoot. Lungs may burst, he thinks. They've made it upstairs, lungs a bit lighter when he sees Emma laying on the bed. She's clammy though, sweating. Thankfully the blood seems to have stopped with her clothes; there is little on the sheets.

More pressing is that animal instinct that says, *flee!* But there is only one window, only one way out of the small bedroom and top floor. Straight down.

'Why did we come up here?' he cries in a frenzy.

'You told me to come up here!'

'I didn't tell you to bring *her* up here! Jesus!'

'*Stop* saying that!'

And Emma whimpers and they both stop, catch their breath as best they can, and it is in that second of silence, as hard feet stamp on the floor below, that he sees it. The revolver sits on the table. Must've left it there after he cleaned it. Usually it lives in the barn under a bail in the corner. Never felt comfortable with it in the house; thing always felt wrong, looking like no pistol should. Too heavy and the odd markings made him shiver. Didn't help that the only time he'd seen those markings was on the stolen saddle or the big book the priest left, on the page with the demons scratched out in fading ink. The book Emma'd taught him with the merchants and sultans and demons who love stories. Same markings were on the flintlock she'd given him an age ago.

Before he knows it, the gun's in his hand and he kicks open the door and fires. One of the strangers is all but a foot from the other side, somehow not expecting the shot, somehow flying back harder than the recoil that throws

Sean's hand to the side and the stranger starts turning black, starts flaking away. Sean's back in the room again, door shut, sweat pouring. Don't throw up, he thinks. Just don't throw up that's all you gotta do right now.

And then the door turns black and crumbles away and there is a figure in the hallway, black flame, the shadow of a man, tall and terrible and unbelievable. His hands are raised. He reaches for Sean and he's sure those hands will find him a room's length away. Gun falls from his hand. Bibiana is crying and praying and crossing herself but Sean cannot hear it. Only a low hum and growing pulse can he hear, his world all a purple shimmer. The dark, flaming hands reach out.

'Challa!' comes a wailing voice. Emma screams in her language, the tongue of the desert. 'Wait! We will tell you a story! We will tell you!' Emma screeches, her voice cracking from the bed.

The hum and throb cease. The figure is a man again. A masked stranger with a low hat and a painted face and a gun on his hip.

'By God, I must kill you as you killed mine. One life for another,' it says.

Emma, pale and shuddering, sits up. 'No. Let us tell you a story. It will be wonderful, from far away. Then you will let us live.'

The stranger steps into the room, the rest shaking and waiting, and like a child the stranger sits on the floor, legs crossed. Its twin is dead, the body gone, the third is off in the grass and the hills.

'I will deem if this story is worth your life. But you cannot have what was taken from me.'

A horse whinnies far away. The others don't hear it but Sean knows. It is Good Heart. Taken. The word crashes down on his head, just as Emma looks to him for this story that will save their lives. It's not to do at all with that necklace from Jack. That debt's been paid long ago, back in the sand and the heat. Killed Jack for it, or for whatever it meant. They're here for his killing of that rider so long ago...and for taking the horse as belonged to him.

Manages to pull it together somehow. There's a calm when the pieces start to take shape and he says, 'A story. Yeah, a story,' and wracks his brain for every tall tale he ever heard, every Indian legend ever came across a bar top. Strange fate, living a full life and placing that life in the hands of a story, but finding no stories to tell from such a life.

'I'll tell you a tale,' he begins. But there is nothing. The stranger remains calm, legs crossed, eyes half-shut. But there is nothing. Sean sweats, fears, his heart races and all he can think of is the horse. And then he speaks.

'I'll tell you a tale of a boy who wished only to have a horse.'

♘

'The older folk of his people, proud warriors all, rode horses over seas of green grass and hunted beasts twice the size of a horse. Three times!' Stops to lick his lips. 'His father was a hunter and warrior; his uncles; even his grandmother had hunted and killed bears for sport, for boredom when the children were reared, they said. And so this boy wanted a horse for himself, for his own, to care for and love and one day ride into battle and into the hunt.

'Each day he would go to the water and listen to the stream. He could hear the rocks chirping. They chirped and sang in their faraway language and told him things, though he could not understand them. Seemed important just the same. And the water drew him pictures all of wavy lines and shade crests and they spoke to him as well, to the deep places beyond words and thoughts. And the mud between his toes and under his nails felt their way into his skin and up his arms and into his heart and fed his insides, all the while the wind brushed him gently and said his name in breathy whispers. And he thought of horses.

'On such a day as he thought best, a cooler day and a softer, when his heart nearly broke for want of his own horse to care for, the notion came to him: he would make his own horse! And the boy listened to the wind and the rocks and the water and soon, with brief apology, dug his hands into the mud. Sun westered and gave him light and all day long he moulded the mud as the potters did. First legs then a body then a tail then the head, high and proud. He gave his mud pony strong legs to ferry him over the plains; bright eyes to see the way; used sticks to carve a strong face to frighten the hunted beasts; and a mane, wavy and great, for his pride. Now, when he came to the stream to listen and wait, he had his horse to feed and water and pat and brush. He brought it hay and grass and such as it would eat. And though it never moved or bowed its head, the feed was gone whenever he returned.

'Each day he would do this and on such a day as he thought best, a day when Sun slept behind white clouds so as not to blind him and the wind was softer and cooler, he lingered too long and slept. Going back to his home he found that the herds of beasts had moved on and the people had gone. "What will I do?" he said to the sky. "I have no horse to carry me and I can never catch my people with only my feet, lest they grow wings!" And he sat in the ground and wept for two days. He wept until he craved the comfort of the rocks in the water and of his horse. He sat by the water as he always did, his head in his hands, fret and worry overtaking him. And then a strange thing happened. He felt a soft, cold nuzzle on his neck. Looking up the boy saw no one else, only his mud pony, still and quiet. When it happened again and he looked again, he heard a voice.

'"Child, why do you cry?" But he saw no one.

'"Who is there?" said he. His horse's head moved. It tilted to and fro and then looked at him with those muddy eyes.

'"I am, your mud pony," it said. "And I ask again, why do you cry?"

'The boy marveled for a moment and replied. "The people have gone and left me and I must catch them. They are chasing the herds over the plains."

'The mouth moved and flaked as the pony spoke, "A trifle!" it said proudly.' Sean stifled a laugh himself. Never fancied he'd be a storyteller, but this one was special. Only heard it once but it stuck with him. He'd told it to Emma before but not like this.

'"We shall go as quickly as you like!" said the pony. "Come, boy."

'And the boy smiled. Muddy face, tear-streaked, broke almost in two, the smile was so big. He climbed the pony easily and felt his heart would twist for the joy of it, this wonderful dream. The mud pony, flaking as he went, walked and cantered and then ran fast as the wind. Over hills and across the plains and through the grass he sped, Sun hardly moving for his haste. The boy would point and the horse would move to follow his direction, the clear signs of a great many people on the move. They went over rocks and little streams that surely would break a pony made of mud, but didn't. Even before Sun westered they spied the camp, and all the people were there with their horses. A beast was on the spit.

'The mud pony stopped in the valley before the camp. "Why do you stop?" asked the boy, "For I wish for all to see you! The finest horse on the plains!"

'"I cannot come, boy. My road ends here."

'And the boy dismounted and frowned a curious frown. "But why?"

'"Who would believe a horse made of mud could carry you so far so fast?" it said. Before the boy could argue, the pony neighed. The wind came and blew it to pieces and scattered its body here and there so that all the plains would know the fastest horse there ever had been. And the boy did not cry, nor did he wish to, for who else could say they had ridden a horse made of mud and made a journey of days in one?'

Ω

The stranger does not move. The stillness in that little room a horror far greater than its black flame. Emma had fallen asleep, taken under by her wounds, and Bibiana was wrenched from the little comfort of her husband's story, so lovingly told. Sean waits, trying to keep his heart in his chest, his bowels from twisting more. As if from waking slumber, the stranger stands and turns and without a word leaves the room.

Stillness grows thick and heavy and burdensome, unwilling to leave with the stranger. An unwelcome guest loathe to take its leave. And so they wait. In fear.

20. HOPE

Seems like hours that they wait and eventually they sleep, overtaken by exhaustion. Man and wife clamor onto the small bed and fall under, sandwiching the girl they love with their bodies, not caring for what's happened or what's to come, for the blood and the sweat. Too tired to do so.

It's late afternoon when the sun wakes them through the western window. If sun hadn't then the cry would have. Sean bolts upright, hearing it again; the shrill neigh of a horse. Sees his wife and child on the bed, stirring. Doesn't wake them but steps carefully over the charred remains of the door and downstairs. He half expects the house to be destroyed but all is as it should be save the overturned table and the broken window. Hears it again and trots to the front door.

Sean looks around the coming gloam but cannot see the source nor place it with his ears. There. A rustling to his right. Runs, barefoot, through the dry grass and beyond the few trees to the base of the most northerly hill of his property, newly dug for the planting of vineyards. At the top is one man and a horse unwilling to concede its will, fighting, black against the setting sun. Good Heart's neighing and stamping and tugging against the reins. Must've given them a hell of a chase today and she still won't back down to the commands, frayed edges of which reach Sean's ears. Whispers in a horrible tongue.

Swears he sees it: white light glimmering off the horse like a flame but it's dimming; dark smoke from the stranger smothering it. Rubs his eyes and the vision passes and his legs, tired and angry, carry him up the hill. He can't stop. Can't stop his foeman any more than he can stop his feet from going to his horse, the greatest horse he'd known. It's unwinnable but the loss is inconceivable.

And yet it's clear.

He steps in between Good Heart and the stranger who is still chanting in low gutturals. He releases the reins as if expecting Sean, lifting no hand to him, and Sean takes Good Heart by the muzzle. Strokes her like she's his own, saying sweet things, wishing he had peppermints for her.

'Just, just wait a minute here,' he whimpers.

'No,' commands the soft voice behind him. Feels it more than hears it, a worm wriggling up his back. 'You know what must be done. Your life is bought back by our mercy and the exchange. This belongs to us. She is forfeit.'

Wishes he could cry but there are no tears, nor time for them. Thinks of the terror of the black flame back in the house. No way out of this corner. No more running or fighting. No more stories. Only goodbyes.

'Time to let you go, I expect, Good Heart. I took you... no, I stole you. Don't believe they'll treat you like we did. Don't know what in the goddam world they'll treat you like and by God it ain't fair. Ain't fair a lick. But the choice is clear. I can fight for you and lose my family, lose my soul, or let you go and maybe find some peace. I dabbled in affairs beyond my reckoning when I took you, when I shook hands with Jack, but by God you were worth the fear and trouble.'

Horse grows calm, tail even swishes. Nuzzles the man

with her white snouts, even licks his hair giving him a quiet assurance.

'Christ,' moans Sean. He breathes and sighs and bites his lip. 'Fare thee well, horse. We'll keep your gift safe.'

Doesn't turn or speak. Lowers his head and the reins are taken from him and there is darkness about his vision. Hears the horse being led away, hears the crunch of grass and clump of hoof and listens, grasps at the sounds until they fade and there is only, in the murmur of coming night, a light pairs of footsteps.

'Sean!' cries his wife.

Lifts his head and midway up the hill is Bibiana, arms around a shuffling Emma. Looks blankly, carelessly at them, then returns to himself, casts aside misery and helps them up.

'Sean, what happened? Why are you out here?'

He only turns to face the setting sun, and there before them in the valley, burning orange between dead hilltops, is the horse and rider. They move slowly, as if the day-light will await their command. An unhappy pair bound together by fate and whatever powers the earth knows. Shadows blend to become one and stretch in the light, an awful truth of what is meant to be, though it strains against the right and wrong of the heart.

Sean expects Emma to tear off her bandage and race after her horse, to curse ground and sky and demand her back, but she is too weak. She collapses against her mother, puts hand to face and weeps. Each sob is a pain but she cannot stop, the grief of this final loss not delaying. But it is made light and carried by a force beyond her control, for there is another neigh, another thumping of hooves.

Up the hill comes Copa in the lead. Behind him is a wobbling filly, sterling in the orange light of dusk. Sean battles tears now, brushing his hand lightly against the young horse. The animal bobs playfully, then perhaps senses the solemnity. She meanders to Emma, nuzzles her, and the girl, with a final inch of strength, wraps her arms around the horse's neck. The tears stop. It is Good Heart's foal, not two weeks old. 'Amal,' Emma had said when she was born, and so that was what they called her. And upon that horse rode a great deal: a hope for the future and a heavy burden, a hole of loss to fill and herds to mind and a ranch to keep. But she was strong, walking and trotting quicker than any foal Sean had seen or heard of.

Amal would grow and light would reign before her and shadow shed behind her. No more night-shadows haunted the ranch. The vines grew fat and sweet and the milk of autumn was bottled and all would sit round the table; the line of Good Heart would go on, tame and yet untamed, kept and yet free; and a life was made, full and rich, the more beautiful for the taint of pain and terror it had known. Never again would Sean cross the sea and face the desert, for there was darkness, he said, buried in the sand. Emma never agreed with her adopted father on that score, and Bibiana went with her in years to follow, to see the little village at the edge of the sea of sand and to listen for a horse's cry on the desert wind, and know that it is like any other place. Light and dark, mingled with the confusion of man.

ACKNOWLEDGEMENTS

This story is the product of a lot of encouragement. Thank you to Lauren, Sarah, Krista, Terrence, and Tom for your thoughtful input and for pushing me to think this thing through.

Thank you to all the backers...

About the Author

Derek A. Kamal lives in Marietta, Georgia with his wife and two daughters. He writes games and books and hopes to publish many more. His previous works include:

Homes, a Novel (2016)

The Dig: A Roleplaying Game (2016)

Heavy Metal Thunder Mouse, a Game (2018)

www.ingramcontent.com/pod-product-compliance
Lightning Source LLC
Chambersburg PA
CBHW032119170626
46808CB00006B/2016